THE SOCIABLE GHOST

THE SOCIABLE GHOST

OLIVE HARPER

Originally published in 1905.

Published by Wildside Press.

Visit us online at wildsidepress.com.

INTRODUCTION
KARL WURF

Olive Harper was the pen name of Ellen Burrell D'Apery, born in 1842 in Tunkhannock, Pennsylvania. She grew up in California, where life was rough. As a child, she faced dangers like disease and wildlife and even lost her sister to diphtheria. Despite these hardships, she loved reading and learning, and she spoke out against anything she found hypocritical or snobby.

At age fifteen, she married an older man named George Gibson. The marriage was unhappy—he became abusive and she later divorced him. Around the same time, she fell ill and was left using crutches for life. She supported herself and her three children through business ventures before she turned to writing.

Once she began writing, she found success quickly. She worked as a journalist and poet for newspapers across the country. She also lectured in public with wit and honesty, sometimes even on adult themes. Later, she became a novelist, writing mysteries and detective stories, early science-fiction, and even novelizations—novels based on plays.

Her work shows influences from early speculative and supernatural romance. In *A Fair Californian* (1889), she imagines a lost civilization under the Earth, a hollow-Earth society with skill, immortality, and even travel to other worlds. In *The Show Girl* (1902) and *The Sociable Ghost* (1903), she again blends the real world with underground realms, unseen beings, or ghostly gatherings beneath a churchyard.

She also produced many novelizations of popular plays in the early 1900s—like *The Gambler of the West, Bertha, the Sewing Machine Girl*, and *The Shoemaker*—often adapting melodramatic scripts into novels.

Here are five recommended works by her, aside from *The Sociable Ghost*:

A Fair Californian (1889)
The Show Girl: Or, the Cap of Fortune (1902)
The Shoemaker (novelization, 1907)

Bertha, the Sewing Machine Girl (1906)
The Gambler of the West (novelization, 1906)

Harper's writing blends journalistic clarity, imaginative settings, and melodrama. She holds a place in early American speculative and detective fiction, and her background as a rugged California pioneer and frank journalist adds depth to her stories.

CHAPTER I
THE BEGINNING OF THE ACQUAINTANCE

AT THE NORTHWESTERN END of Trinity Church stands a clump of bushes under a tree, and lying under both bushes and tree is a large, flat stone with the inscription quite effaced. It is the entrance to one of the old family vaults. Beneath this dense shrubbery in the darkness at night sat a young man. The hour was so late that even in that busy neighborhood the lights were few and far between, except in the tall newspaper offices up the street.

Few people could be seen on the great thoroughfare which but a few hours before had been so animated. Stillness reigned save for the occasional train of cars now and then whizzing by at the back, and the Broadway cars shooting along at great and uninterrupted speed in front.

The young man was not ill nor out of employ, as the notebook and pencils in his pocket would show. Yet he was plainly out of sorts with everything.

A little dog came sniffing around him and he kicked it viciously, and a starved kitten crept timidly up to him, whereat he picked a piece of stone from the slab and threw it at the little creature which, frightened, scampered away in the darkness.

Aroused thus from his reverie, the young man looked and felt more miserable than ever. He was surprised at himself, for this was the first time in his life that he had ever made a movement to harm an animal. His conscience pricked him and he did not like the sensation.

From all this it may be inferred that the young man was in love, and that was the truth; and worse than all, the girl of his choice was now as unattainable as one of the stars in the Milky Way. First of all, she was the only daughter of a millionaire, and secondly, she was to be married the next day to an impecunious nobleman from sunny France. Thirdly, she had eyes only for the grand title. And that was why this young man sat alone in the darkest corner of Trinity churchyard, kicking dogs and stoning cats.

That very day his chief had given him an assignment to go and write a description of the wedding presents. He had turned in his copy, and not waiting to find out if there was anything else to do, went out, and with the instinct of a hurt dog, had chosen the darkest spot he knew of, and had crept down to this place, which even in daylight is gloomy, prepared to suffer as much as he wished to, unknown to anyone. If he went home he must see his adoring mother. He was not prepared for that. He felt that he could not bear the scrutiny of her soft but penetrating glance until he had gotten over the worst. He knew well that she would see his trouble, even though he said no word, and that she would wait for him to speak. But, even this unspoken sympathy was more than he could endure. He intended to fight it out alone, now and in the darkness, shut out from human kind and curious scrutiny.

A fine old pipe and a paper of tobacco, not yet opened, and a box of matches were in his pocket, but he was in no mood for the soothing influence of the weed. In another pocket was a flask of good whiskey which he always carried for such emergencies as might arise in his profession as a reporter, but it was full and untouched. He had forgotten that he had it.

The noises of the great city were settling down to a soft hum as it approached midnight. The trains and electric cars were fewer now, while the throbbing of the newspaper presses away up on Park Row sounded clear and distinct in his ears as the other noises ceased. The sweet calm of a mild May night fell unconsciously upon him and brought with it a feeling almost of resignation.

Suddenly he became aware that he was not alone. Amazed and bewildered, he saw that the old graveyard was waking up, and that from every grave issued a shade which took form as it rose fully free from the earth.

A shadowy figure quite near him appeared entirely ignorant of his presence, and as soon as his cerements were free from the mold of the grave from which he had come, gave an audible sniff, shook himself so that his bones rattled like a bag of dry oyster shells, and as he did so said:

"Zounds and pea blossoms! What wouldn't I give for a good pipe full of tobacco! I've a notion to stay dead."

Saying this the loose-jointed ghost threw one leg over his tombstone and began to drum on it with his heels, while he folded his bony arms with supreme disgust.

The newspaper man, now all alert to the situation, hurriedly opened the paper of tobacco and filling his pipe, which was of that warm, rich hue of brown so dear to the heart of the smoker as the result of many hours of solitude, and much copy, he lighted it and sent out a couple of whiffs to pave the way for his voice which followed the puffs of smoke. The ghost still sat drumming with his heels on the stone and watched the operation.

"If I—may I—offer you my pipe?" stammered the young man.

"You may, indeed, and be sure of the thanks of a man who has not smoked for so long that he has almost forgotten how it tastes."

The ghost sighed so heavily that the rags fluttered around as he drew himself up with dignity, at the same time covering his breast bone with the morsels of his shroud. He received the pipe most graciously and enjoyed it with infinite gusto, though, to be sure, the smoke seemed to ooze out afterwards from all over his angular anatomy.

The little heart of fire glowed brightly in the bowl of the pipe, and as the rich cloud of smoke gradually enveloped the ghost, it told more eloquently than words could have done of his enjoyment. The newspaper man stood ready to fill it up again, and it suddenly occurred to him that possibly the contents of the small flask in his pocket might prove acceptable, so he made bold to offer it, saying:

"I have a little old whiskey, if you ever indulge—"

"Indulge! Dear sir, you are a Christian! I have not had a snifter for—as many years as I have been dead. Tears enough to float a seventy-four gun ship have bedewed my grave, but nobody has ever thought of pouring out a little good rum. Ah, there is a flavor about rum so rich and fine that it makes one think of all the molasses in the world boiled down into one bottle. Here's to your health; your very good health, the health of your wife, your children, your mother, and hoping that your bottle may never be empty!"

With every fresh sentiment the ghost lifted the bottle to his mouth, and at last handed that and the pipe back with evident reluctance. The pipe was now cold.

"Would you care to smoke again?" asked the young man.

"I would indeed, my good sir. I cannot tell you the comfort you have given me on this occasion, an occasion only too trying to the most hardened ghost."

"May I ask the nature of it?"

"You may; you may. I owe you that much. But, before I do, let me move around so that I cannot see that fellow's headstone. It makes me sick. Just see that epitaph. I knew the chap, and all about him. The epitaph tells how brave he was in the Mexican war where he fell a hero. Instead of dying like a hero, he ran like a whitehead—he did—and caught his foot in a vine and fell into a cactus bush and was kicked to death by a Roman-nosed mule with one loose shoe. It was that loose shoe that did the business."

Here the ghost fell to puffing again with a vigor born of vexation and disgust. The newspaper man now saw that there were many other forms quite as unsubstantial as this one walking around slowly. He noticed also that they kicked vigorously at some of the headstones as they passed, and that they all appeared to have and show a special hatred for some dark objects scattered among the graves. The young man could not resist the desire to know why the other ghosts seemed to be so angry. The ghost who was still smoking with evident pleasure, said:

"Oh, the usual thing."

"And what is that, if I may ask?"

"Oh, just as if it is not enough to be dead and not have your passport yet! Here come a lot of fools and stick flowers over your grave. It is true that we do not have so much to complain of in this respect as some of the newer cemeteries do. The most of us have been here for so long that we have no relatives to come here and leave them, and the public thinks it is quite honor enough to be buried here. Other cemeteries may be forgotten or removed, but this one is as solid as the rock of Gibraltar. It is honeycombed about as much too. And there are flowers enough growing in their proper places without sticking more around. We don't care so much for sentiment as people seem to think we do. We have learned the value of it. We have grown practical."

The newspaper man held out his hand for the pipe to fill it again, gently asking the ghost to tell him what this special occasion might be, adding that he would be very grateful for anything that the ghost might be willing to impart, as probably he would never have a better chance to learn.

The other ghosts sauntered along, looking enviously at this one as he sat there smoking vehemently and reflecting. It actually appeared that the ghosts could see and that they looked at him, though in the very nature of things they ought not to be able to see without eyes. Their efforts to appear entirely unconcerned while the favored one sat smoking were funny, or would have been so under any other circumstances.

The young journalist had mentally christened this as the Sociable Ghost, and he waited silently, observing him while he did so, and pondered on the delight of the smoker as he in time became conscious of the glances of envy and overwhelming smoke-hunger of the other ghosts. They evidently would have done anything for just one whiff at that pipe, but they saw that there was nothing to hope for, and that they were confronting another bloated monopoly. But they all ranged themselves in line with apparent carelessness, so that the night wind should waft the smoke toward them. They sniffed the smoke eagerly and looked as though they would like to annihilate the smoker.

Apparently unnoticing and unconcerned, the sociable ghost continued to smoke as though reflecting on what he should say to this young man, and possibly it occurred to him that if he told all there was to say too soon, the young man might go away, and there was still quite a lot of tobacco in the paper, and some more of the whiskey which he had left in the flask for good manners. He could not jeopardize what might be his last chance.

"There is a sort of sameness here," said the ghost irrelevantly, with a comprehensive wave of the hand, "particularly in the architecture." And then he suddenly kicked at a bone which had attracted his attention, though how it had escaped the attention of Floyd, whose whole life is spent in trying to keep the place immaculately clean is a mystery. The young man thought perhaps the little dog had brought it in. But, however it had come there, it seemed to annoy the ghost greatly. He said angrily:

"There's reverence for you! There's respect and sentiment. When I was a small shaver I regarded a graveyard as a sacred place, and scarcely dared to let my little feet fall for fear they might weigh too heavily on the sainted dead below. 'Sainted dead!' Now that is a good one, too! Well, perhaps familiarity does breed contempt. If you will excuse me for mentioning it, my pipe is out," remarked the ghost rather abruptly. The young man filled it, and at the same time the thought intruded itself into his mind that the ghost had said "My pipe." The ghost took it gracefully and after a couple of puffs said:

"If you like, we will walk around a little while I smoke this last pipe, for I shall soon have sights to show you, as well as things to tell, and must hurry before we begin the carnival."

"Begin what?" asked the young man a little nervously.

"Well, we have a sort of convention of all the ghosts of this city and some delegations from other places, some from quite a distance, I believe. We are to have a dance after some speech-making and a banquet. There will also be some general amusements such as are permitted in good society. After that we do our penance—that is some regard it in that light, but I do not for it makes the stone lie heavy over my head."

As the Sociable Ghost said that he waved his hand indefinitely and stood up on his skeleton feet and prepared to walk.

"As we go along I will tell you many things that never came to your knowledge, and they may be of service to you in after life. If I had known all that I am going to show you and tell you tonight before I died, I might have done some things and not done others, and so shortened my probation a good while. I then would never have been stuck under this lying stone."

In the meantime the number of ghosts grew larger so rapidly that it seemed there would soon be room for no more. The ghost said:

"The most of the ghosts that you see here tonight above ground are invited guests, and they come because the march of civilization as you call it, has left them no place where they might hold a reunion of their own, for it is only in settled cemeteries that there can be such a function as you shall see here tonight—that is if you wish to remain."

The newspaper man hastily signified that he would indeed like to be present at such a function. Up to the present time in his career as a reporter he had never flinched from anything in the way of sight-seeing, and after having witnessed so much that was strange and hazardous he was not going to flinch now. The ghost continued:

"The whole place is honeycombed with vaults which we can at will transform into a place befitting the occasion. This is done by means of certain powers given us, but before I go on I wish you to take particular notice of my headstone. Why, I will tell you later. I know all the ghosts belonging to this place and many more, and whatever I may say about them will be truthful history and no one will say that I have ever belied him."

The young man hastened to remark that he was sure of that, adding that he had always heard of the chivalric manner in which the men of the past generations spoke of others, and especially he admired the reverence which they showed towards all women, which was very beautiful.

A strange, crackling laugh was the answer to this. It sent the cold chills galloping up and down the reporter's spine. It also checked any further expression of his admiration of bygone manners.

"Young man, you are positively refreshing! We did regard all women except our own and the ugly ones with the greatest consideration. That has been the rule since the world began, and will be unto the end. But to resume. Look now at my headstone. I was a rich man in my day and time and had every reason to expect a fine monument with a weeping willow on it or at least a cherub, and a nice big slab. Just see what I got! It reminds me of one Christmas morning when after I had been extra good for three months hoping to get a bright red sled, I found a copy of Sanford and Merton in my stocking. I wonder I didn't turn out to be a pirate! Maybe I didn't go out behind the barn and tear the thing up, and lie like a little imp when they found out the book was gone. Since then I made it a point to lick every man by the name of Sanford or Merton that I ever met. Fool names, both of them."

"I don't blame you a bit," said the young man with spirit, as the remembrance of much the same experience flitted across his mind. The Sociable Ghost continued:

"Pardon me for interrupting—I am a little out of practice in telling a story. To take up the thread of my narrative. Here you see a measly little slab of red sandstone, and no sign of the little cherub that sits up aloft watching out for the safety of poor Jack. I was a captain and commanded my own ship. She was as fine a vessel as ever rode out a gale. I loved every timber in her hull and every rope on the rigging and every spar and mast and sail as women love their young ones."

"I can quite understand that," assented the young man.

"Well, my ship made me a rich man. My relict, to offset the strict economy that she showed in the matter of stone, had a lot of stuff about my noble qualities and my pious—and all that. So much indeed, that not half shows above ground. All of this makes me just so much work and dirty work. Digging down in it without implements! You may see where it says that I sailed to Liverpool, and so I did, once or twice, but the most of my voyages were to the West Indies and to Africa. I brought cargoes of rum and molasses for the merchants who were in the business here then, and who were not ashamed of working in their own warehouses, and whose descendants today put on many grand airs. They talk about their ancestors, as though they had been of some superior clay. I hate airs, and always did. Nine out of ten of these old merchants dealt in either slaves or rum. The slaves came from the coast of Africa. I brought them for the account of these people whose descendants put on the airs. I suppose from the legend on my headstone if I had left any descendants they would have put on quite as many airs. I am glad I did not. As I said, I hate airs."

"I think any right-feeling person does," hazarded the reporter, who was a little in doubt as to the outcome of this conversation.

"I held my wife so close in money matters," continued the ghost reminiscently, "being thrifty, and looking forward to the time when I should be able to stay on shore, that I never let her know how much I had. Later, when she got control of all my earnings she had so profited by my example and teachings that—well, you see what a headstone she gave me. I had done many things for that money—things that I now wish that I had not done. I taught her economy and by George! when she had a chance to pay me in my own coin, she did it and she did it well. Just look at that miserable chunk of old sandstone all covered with a lot of da—I mean a lot of untruthful stuff that will keep me at it I don't know how many years yet. If she had known she could not have revenged herself on me worse. She gave all my clothes and a puncheon of good rum to the fool sculptor, and I am just waiting for him to come down here. If he ever does, I won't do a thing to him but make him think he mistook his vocation and ought to have been a boiler maker and stayed safely in one of his iron-clad boilers."

As the angry ghost delivered himself of this speech, he somehow took on such a fierce expression, shown more in attitude than feature—since he had no features—that the young man was sincerely glad that he had not been guilty of carving the objectionable stuff on the fast crumbling stone. As they walked along the ghost continued:

"Now, take notice that this stone has all the epitaph rubbed out. The name only remains, and that proves that he was a pretty good sort. Here is another where the epitaph is all gone except the date. Now that is a good start, isn't it?"

The young man murmured something about it seeming so, though he was entirely in the dark about it. Still he knew enough to keep still and let the ghost tell his story in his own way and in his own time. Many a time he had managed to secure a fine story for his paper from someone who had declared that he had nothing to say by judiciously keeping silence, curbing his curiosity and inquisitiveness, and speaking only when absolutely necessary. He began to feel that he was going to get something tonight not often given to mortals, and he mentally arranged the headlines of the story, for of course he would sell it. Every other experience save one had been made to yield him so many dollars, and it was natural that this strange meeting should appeal to him only as a scoop beyond the power of any mortal to equal. So he discreetly awaited the pleasure of his ghostly companion.

He wondered if the pebbles hurt the ghost's feet. He felt a little delicate about mentioning it, particularly as he could have proposed no remedy even if the pebbles did hurt. Soon the ghost stopped by a rather small headstone, and in a reminiscent manner said, between the delicious whiffs of smoke:

"I well remember when the fashion for these cherubs went out and fancy monuments with weeping willows on them came in. I had not been dead then very long, and I was wondering which I would get and thinking what a luminous old gump I was not to have made some provision for just such a contingency. By dying suddenly my widow had things her own way, and a pretty mess she has made of it as you see. Well; cherubs went out and weeping women in weeds standing over funeral urns took their places. I had thought that the new ones looked more dignified and were superior, but since then I have come to see these cherubs as they are. Where there are cherubs there is not much epitaph. Have you ever seen these cherubs? No? Well come then, and take a good look at them for they are worth the trouble. Some of them will fill you with envy to think you cannot have one right away to watch over your slumber—I don't think,"

This last was said with an indescribably waggish leer, and the reporter began to think he was on the right road to a new experience and that this man who had been so long dead still could see the humorous side of it all, and that would certainly be from a new viewpoint.

They walked along until they came to one part of the cemetery where there seemed to have been an epidemic of headstones with cherubs on them. The ghost stopped before one of them and said:

"Just take a look at this cherub and see the mouth—or rather where the mouth once was—and notice how it is all worn away, that is if the sculptor did not die before he had finished his work. Here is another where the mouth is half gone, and the expression is half a mocking smile on one side and nothing at all on the other. Some have faces round and others have long ones; some smile and others have the lips drawn down almost to the chin in a lugubrious line each side of the face. Just notice this one! The shape of the face is like that of a Bartlett pear with the big end down, and around the head is what the artist fondly believed to be a halo of glory; but it looks more like a bunch of oakum tied to a ruffled nightcap. The oakum is supposed to represent the living flame of sacred fire. And just catch onto the wings! And note the general expression! These things were much admired in those days, and were considered the highest form of expression of poetic thought. I think I even complained just now that none had been put on my headstone, but after all I'm blamed—no blessed glad of it for they are silly and they do grate on my sense of the fitness of things, and they might after all interfere with my passport. Oh, yes; I will tell you about that later. Just now I want to show you around a little, for probably you will never again have an opportunity like this."

Here the reporter caused a slight interruption in the conversation by handing the ghost the flask with a quiet grace which completely captivated his heart, that is, the ghost of a heart. The ghost took a few swallows and with a Chesterfieldian bow returned it to the young man and then continued his running commentaries on the headstones.

"Now we come to a new departure in cherubs. You see this one is not very well supplied with flesh, and is cut to represent a skeleton's head. I have noticed in many churchyards that it is considered quite the thing to preach sermons to the living on the mutability of human affairs, and therefore these things are put on the stones. I think the most of them are put there out of spite because the person down below had to die. I know quite a number of ghosts who have told me that they left instructions for their own epitaphs. So you see the ghosts get some comfort out of the gruesome warnings, but I doubt that anyone living was ever scared into repentance by them. I know one old fellow who gets so mad every time he hears people up above read his epitaph and laugh at the time-honored words of 'As I am now, so you must be; prepare for death and follow me—'"

Here the reporter could not restrain his tongue and he asked if it were possible for the dead lying in their graves to really hear, and know what was passing. The ghost replied:

"Oh, yes; we know all that goes on above ground, that is if it interests us enough to make us care to take the trouble to learn. We each find out what we most care about, much as you who are not dead do, and we talk it over at our hour of release."

"And that I suppose is between the hours of twelve and one?"

"My young friend, you are behind the age. There was a time when people believed that ghosts could walk only at the hour you mention, but there is one night when we can walk from sunset to one o'clock, which you see brings us into another day. We can walk, run, dance or do anything we like, within certain limitations. You have happened here on the only night in the year when we can do this. We have been going the rounds below ever since the sun went down and now we are coming up as you see. We leave our coffins and go about—and in short—you shall see it all tonight."

Here the ghost gave a sniff of disgust and anger, and pointing at a headstone, said:

"Now, just look at that! They have gone and 'restored' that headstone and had all that fulsome epitaph recut in it. And, they thought they were doing a meritorious action, and that will give that poor fellow no end of trouble to get it out again. And, he cannot get his passport until he does. And here is another similar case. See this stone? Well, only today the descendants of this man—take notice that I say who has slept, for he is wide awake enough now and hopping mad—came and gave orders that the inscription be restored. Poor fellow! He has been at that trying to scrub it out ever since 1796. It seems that some of the families who have so little to be proud of in this generation try to make it up by piling more misery on their dead ancestors, just to show that they had ancestors with such very flattering records. Bah!"

"He must be rather old?" hazarded the reporter with a desire to learn something besides the opinion of the ghost regarding the inscriptions, whereupon the ghost turned sharply around and said with some little show of asperity:

"He was only about forty and he is the same now. Ghosts cannot grow older, for there is nothing for them to grow with. Here is the grave of Alexander Hamilton. Later I shall show you what he looks like now."

Saying this the ghost seemed to be absorbed in reflection for a few moments. Suddenly he spoke:

"What a pity that you have no more whiskey. There are several persons here tonight who would so enjoy a good snifter. The worst feature about our banquets is that all our food and drink are as unsubstantial as we are."

"I could go across the way and get some, if you will wait for me," said the young man eagerly, for it occurred to him that he would like to see the effect of a generous allowance of real whiskey on the ghosts, and there were apparently legions of them now strolling around among the graves and through the church.

"Never mind for this time," said the ghost. "I have had all that is good for me, and I always knew when I had enough. Besides, I would like to take a rise out of some of these fellows tonight. You see, it is a great thing for one so long dead to have any friends left alive anyhow and above all one who knows enough to bring any creature comforts like the pipe and whiskey."

The young man bowed, and said no more on that subject, but he began to think that this ghost was entirely too prolix.

"Notice, my young friend," said the ghost, confidentially, "as they strolled along toward the south side of the churchyard; "all these stones are set facing the sunrising. Now, some might think this was done on account of the formation of the ground, but it is not so, for it would have been just as easy to have faced them all south, north, east or west. This is simply the last lingering remains of the old heathen custom and belief that the rising sun represents the resurrection of the dead. The ancients also believed in pouring out drink offerings and libations, and, my friend, they were nearer right than we are with all our boasted civilization. Nothing can be of benefit to the dead, unless it is spirits which are ethereal in themselves, and smoke which is evanescent, and almost intangible. I assure you there are times when we could appreciate a glass of good rum. That being a spirit in itself, we assimilate it easily and enjoy it thoroughly. But our civilization does not believe in offering libations to the dead, more's the pity. I knew an old heathen once who had been buried hundreds of years, and he used to make us all as mad as hops when he told us how his descendants, as is the custom there, came regularly to his grave and poured out good spirits. By George! It almost made me wish that I had been one myself."

After that sentiment forcibly expressed, the couple walked along in silence for a short distance, and the ghost stubbed his toe against the slab covering the Barclay vault. This bore the date of 1762 in measurably clear letters. The good-natured ghost seemed suddenly changed in regard to the mildness of his disposition, as he hopped around on one bony foot and said things, some of them sounding like a word beginning with a big D and ending with a little n. The newspaper man bowed his head over the tomb of brave Lawrence, and had a severe coughing fit to cover up his unholy amusement, and whether it was that the ghost was too much occupied in rubbing his toe, or whether he really did not see it, this danger passed, and the ghost turned and limped toward the front of the church and across the porch. As he did so, he said:

"Drat that toe! I nearly put it out of joint! I despise airs anyhow, and folks that think themselves too good to have just plain graves, and go and dig vaults and leave the slabs lying right in one's path. If I had them aboard my ship I'd fix them. I'd stow them so close that when they got out they would think that a six-foot grave was an extended plain or a rolling prairie. I am afraid I shall have to tie that toe on, for I am sure it must be loose."

"Can I be of any assistance?" asked the reporter.

"Nah, you can't. Excuse me if I am short, but the damn thing hurts."

"I had an impression that after one is dead there could be no more bodily pain—that all suffering of the body is over," hazarded the newspaper man.

"Well, get rid of that impression in short order," said the ghost as he sat down on the edge of the porch and struggled to tear off a piece of his shroud to tie up his toe. "We can suffer as long as there is anything material of us left to suffer, and also mentally as long as things go wrong that we left behind us when we died. Zounds! How that toe hurts!"

The young man expressed his sympathy so warmly that that and perhaps somewhat less of pain calmed the ghost so that he took up his interrupted conversation.

"If you use your eyes, young man, you may see here the present homes of many persons who have made the history of New York; yes, even of America. Many of the names are known in every household in the land, and streets have been named for most of them. Among them you will find the names of the founders of the old families, though to be sure, when I come to think of it, many of them have long since received their passports. You therefore will not see them tonight. But you may see some of the Van Dams, Kissams, Ludlows, Moores, Vestrys, Goelets, Desbrosses, Duanes, Worths, Lispenards, Jays, Hulls, Jones, Dominicks, Bleeckers, de Peysters, Murrays, Chambers, Watts, Kings, Munroes, Leroys and a whole lot more. I can't remember them all just now. But, a man has got to be something before he gets a street named after him. Some of the old members of these families were not so rich as their descendants are today. There were no millionaires in my time in New York."

CHAPTER II
THE REPORTER MEETS THE LEADER OF THE FOUR HUNDRED

THE SOCIABLE GHOST AND the newspaper man continued their walk though the ghost still limped painfully. The reporter tried to bring himself to offer his arm for the ghost to lean upon, but somehow he could not seem to care to get too close to the living skeleton as he mentally considered him. Still he would not willingly have dispensed with his company. Finally the ghost took up the conversation where he had left it off.

"I was not born then, let alone being dead, but I have often conversed with the founders of this mother of churches in this country, and also the founders of those first families at our reunions. You just ought to hear them go on about the extravagance of their descendants. They say that when they were taking up subscriptions for building the new steeple, Joseph Aspinwall gave one pound six, and Oliver Schuyler put down one pound; Mrs. Coddington gave two pounds, while Gilbert Livingstone gave five shillings and six pence. Philip Schuyler donated six shillings, Mrs. Hamilton gave two pounds fifteen shillings, and Rip Van Dam, one pound six shillings, and so on no one giving much, if any more than two pounds. This was while John Cruger was vestry-man with Isaac Decker and Josephus Bayard as co-laborers. I notice that the women were more generous then as now to church matters and needs, and it has always been a question with me why this is so. Now, is it because as a general rule the women did not have to work for the money as the husbands did, and so they did not appreciate its value, or is it because the women are by nature more generous and more religious than men? I heard somewhere once that it was said that it is the women who sustain the churches. Well, I don't care, Wow! That toe twinges!"

All this did not interest the young reporter as much as the ghost seemed to think it should, but politeness forbade him to make any sign. His appetite was whetted for what was to come and he did not wish to destroy his chances. He had a vague idea that he had read something like this in the archives of this old and honored church, while preparing a description of the three hundredth anniversary, but as he saw that the ghost liked to enlighten his ignorance he wisely kept silence. At this moment the ghost said:

"Come on, it will soon be time now. But before we go take one look at the headstone erected to the memory of William Bradford. He was the first Government printer and spent fifty years in the service, and left this world worn out with old age and labor. He printed the first Bible in this country, and his old press is kept as a memorial.

"He was a decent, simple, hardworking chap, and used all his strength in his work. And, he didn't get rich either. Well; maybe you have seen instances of the truly good getting the fool good to sign away their lives for the benefit of the truly good. I put this matter in a mild form, for I am apt to get hot under the collar when I think of how many of the fool-good fellows are bound down to a life of underpaid toil to give others the benefit of it all."

Here the ghost paused impressively, and the reporter bowed seriously as though fully agreeing with him. In fact he did fully agree with the ghost completely, for he knew something of the matter himself in a small way. The ghost resumed:

"When I say the truly good, I mean those who are so very good that the fool-good are blinded by their reputation and so toil for them for next to nothing. I tell you, publishers have no pudding down here, and the religious ones seem to be singled out for special punishment. One man is here tonight who used to run a religious paper. All he paid his writers was one dollar a column, and however hard they tried they couldn't earn over six or seven dollars a week. He made contracts with the poor fellows to write for him alone, so they could not help themselves when he cut down the number of columns. One of these unfortunate men wrote a book while this contract was in force and it made quite a success and blow me! if the religious chap did not go and claim the book, too. How it would have turned out I do not know for the publisher died. I'll show him to you when we go down, that is if you would care to see him."

"You bet I would!" said the reporter with sudden warmth. Whereupon the ghost said in a manner to calm his just anger:

"I don't think they are all so bad. But one thing I have noticed and that is that all the publishers have money, and all the things that money brings, while the great majority of the writers are poor, some of them miserably so. All the religious publishers and editors are down here and rather flock together. They seem to enjoy talking over the tricks of trade. I used to think that I was something of a pirate, too, in my way, and therefore their conversations interested me more probably, than they might otherwise have done. If you were to hear them talk together you would think much less of them than you do now."

"I couldn't!" answered the young man, with emphasis and conviction.

"I will show you another thing tonight that ought to please you if you take any special interest in publishers, and that is what is done with those publishers who make the writers wait for their money until their stories are published. It would be a balm for the hearts of the authors, and I wish you would let the writers know about it. It may be a poor satisfaction for those who die before their stories are published. It has always been a satisfaction to me to whale the fellow that tries to cheat me out of my own, and if I can't whale him to see someone else do it and do it up brown."

"They tell us that we must speak no evil of the dead," said the young man tritely.

"These dead don't wait for anyone to tell what they have done, They think it is all right. What they have to suffer in seeing the papers, or the books they used to work on and about done so much better than they could do while alive! The policies of the whole thing are changed in many cases and that is very bitter. Well, with one last word on this subject I will let them alone. It seems to me that when a man writes a book or a story and offers it for sale, he has the same right to offer it as an artist his picture, or a cabinet-maker to offer his wares, and I can't see why the author should have to wait for his pay any more than the others. If it suits the publisher enough to cause him to buy it the buyer should pay for it. I have heard men tell here how they had had stories accepted for publication and kept there year after year, and then they died before they were published. And, as soon as they did die the publishers used them at once and paid nothing even to the widows. Now, of course, I have no means of knowing much about these matters, but it seems to me to be an outrage if it is true. I used to write poetry on shipboard, at night, and I am sure that I should not have liked this sort of treatment, if it is true."

"Some of them are several times meaner than any you have mentioned. But, show them to me if you please," said the reporter, who had a bone to pick with two or three dead publishers.

"I will. I am sorry for poor Bradford, for they have gone and restored his whole epitaph. He was good to me when I first came down and kindly taught me the rules. It is a bit rough until you have learned the ropes after you are dead."

"Will you excuse me if I ask you a question? I have always been led to think that those who are dead dislike to hear the word dead. They are supposed to prefer to hear, 'passed into spirit life' and 'gone to Summerland' instead. All the mediums use that word, in palliation and instead of the harsher one. Dead, gives one a shock to hear," asked the young man in a laudable desire to learn all he could.

"Poppycock and moonshine!" was the unexpected response. "There is no such thing as a medium. No, sir; they get your money and—do you suppose that one of them could get you the invitation to come down here tonight? You are soon to enter the very doors of ghostdom, but not through the efforts of any medium. No, sir; they trade upon your sense of loss and sorrow when anyone of yours dies, and they foster and encourage your desire to penetrate the mystery of the future life. They get your money by fraud, working upon your best sentiments. They ought to be keelhauled, and should be if I had my way. I'd string them to the yardarm and whack them with a rope's end. If the tie that bound you to anyone you loved is broken by death there is no third party that can come and for a certain sum in cash become the medium of communication between you, and I say, lick the man that tells you different. You are getting this straight from a real ghost. In my warmth I had almost forgotten that you asked if we who are dead dislike to hear anyone say the word Dead. Quite the contrary, for we are dead and it would be very silly to try to disguise the fact, and we do not try to down here. Fact is truth and truth governs down here. Dead we are and dead we stay, and after all I am not sure that we are not quite as well, and sometimes better off, than when alive. If we miss some things we escape others. Well, come on; but before we go let me say that the Trinity ghosts are the hosts tonight and they feel themselves the most aristocratic ghosts in the land, so I wished to caution you so that you would avoid hurting anyone's feelings by seeming to doubt it."

"I shall be very careful, sir, and hope you will be near enough to forewarn me of any possible mistake. I assure you that I appreciate this distinguished honor more than I can say. But, I should like to ask if any of the Vanderbilts will be here tonight?"

"No, young man; there will be no Vanderbilts here tonight. But I can tell you something else that may interest you, and that is where old John Jacob Astor is tonight. You have doubtless heard that the old man was a worker from head to foot. Work was ingrained in his thrifty nature. He wandered all over America to buy up fur skins. For a long time he carried them on his back, so we are told, until his business had grown so that he required help, and could afford to pay for it. Even then he would gladly have carried them all, so great was his instinct of thrift. Then, when he found he could not tie them up alone he bought a baling press. This baling press he came to love. It marked for him the very spirit of progress, though it is a clumsy old thing made of beams and iron levers and screws. To this he confided his ambitions and joys and sorrows. So when his year of dormant waiting is over, like ours, and he is at liberty to amuse himself as he wishes for the few hours before the penance begins, The Master lets him choose between this evening of festivity and his own desire. His ghost is now down in the sub-cellar of the great John Ruszits fur company, where the women of four generations have brought their furs. This company was formed in 1851, and Astor died a few years before. The new Ruszits company must have felt a certain friendship for the old man, though there is no record of their ever dining together, for when the old baling press was about to be sold for junk, at auction, with the rest of the effects of the old fur house, they purchased it and had it set up in the sub-cellar and have carefully preserved it ever since. It is about thirty feet below the surface of the street. It is pretty sure that the present members of the family have no desire to keep it as an heirloom.

"That is about all of the old man's effects left intact, and he is naturally drawn toward it, and now he is standing there in the pungent odor of raw pelts, and turning that baling press for all he is worth and if ghosts can sweat he is sweating now and enjoying himself in the keenest delight."

"I should think he would prefer to spend the evening at the magnificent library which his money gave to the world. That is a noble sight, and I should think he would be glad to get out of the ground for a while."

"My young friend, John Jacob Astor, the founder of that family, loved his business better than money. He could not be hired to leave the old press for all the books there is in it. When he is debarred from his present occupation he puts in his time turning over the raw furs in this place and inhaling their pungent odor, familiar and redolent of the old days. The rest of his time he sleeps and takes the repose which his active spirit would not allow him on earth."

The young newspaper man thought a little about these things and remembered that only a few days ago he had been in this very warehouse where he had seen so much of beauty and value and yet missed seeing this old baling press, and he rather wondered, too, how anyone could prefer the penetrating odor of raw skins to the fresh air of night under the stars. He could understand how the sight and feel of the soft finished garments might appeal to one, but he only said:

"I don't see why the Family should care for a better name and fame than that the old man left—that of an industrious, frugal and honest man—"

Before the young man could finish his sentence he became aware of a perfect cloud of shadowy forms, and all seemed to be gathering around him. He began to wish that he had gone for the whiskey and failed to return. His companion sat on the edge of a tombstone from which he had seemed to exude when he first made his appearance.

They had returned to that place while talking and as he did so he rubbed his stubbed toe, and for a few minutes no one said or did anything. At last the ghost said in a sibilant whisper:

"I think there would be time for one more smoke if you would be so good. The guests are gathering fast and I will smoke fast, too."

The young man hastily filled the pipe with the last of the tobacco and the ghost smoked it and handed it back, saying:

"The tobacco is nearly all powder and does not smoke so well as the rest. No, no, I am not blaming you, but only saying that one of my experiences in life has been that when we do not use the good things of life with moderation we are sure to find the last lacking in flavor. Now, I could not resist one last smoke when I knew I might never have another, and in so doing I drained the cup to the dregs, so to speak—"

"Excuse me for interrupting, but if I am alive next year, and you will tell me how I can find you, I will come and bring such creature comforts as you may wish to have. If you will tell me—"

"I thank you with all my heart, and would suggest that the liquid refreshment might be rum, good Jamaica rum. I acquired a taste for that, and beyond that and a good smoke I can ask for nothing for it may have occurred to you that I have no need for food.

"We are now about to go below for the banquet and general reunion of such of us as have become acquainted. There will be some guests from Derby, Conn., and some of their relatives, and there will be some Revolutionary soldiers, and quite a number of tramp ghosts. A few sailors will also be here. They have been lying in a forgotten place over in Brooklyn and they are now being rooted out of there for someone wants to build a house. And I notice there seven old fellows who have been lying under the Hall of Records. There was once a cemetery there and many more are there but I shall not be the one to go and tell where. It is bad enough to be waiting for your passport without having to be a tramp ghost beside. Many of the old Revolutionary heroes lie there and in the language of a poet: 'The knights are dust, And their good swords are rust; Their souls are with the saints, we trust.'

"Ah, well! Ladies will also grace the feast. The only unpleasant thing is that we have never been able to sweep away class distinctions, and pride of birth. And, I must confess that I am as bad as anyone, for whenever I see a sailor I just ache to send him to the forecastle, and of course there is no such place here. You have heard of the ruling passion being strong in death. It remains with us much as it was before we died, and it seems as if nothing can be of much moral or spiritual good until we get our passports."

Just as the newspaper man was about to ask again about the passports, the other ghosts were so near that he waited, and at that moment a tall ghost stood up very straight, and smoothing a lock of imaginary hair from his forehead, said:

"Ladies and gentlemen—." Then he paused and looked so steadily at the young man that he felt his heart sink into his boots, but the tall ghost contented himself with one long regard, and then he continued:

"Ladies and gentlemen, we have met here tonight to fulfill our yearly duty, and to meet in friendly intercourse. I hope you will all have a good time."

As he said this he sat down on the edge of a crumbling headstone and glared around. There were murmurs of approbation and he rose and bowed with as much grace as was possible to a ghost who had scarcely a dozen remnants of his shroud hanging around him. But this absence of raiment did not seem to affect the ghosts in the least, and only one or two appeared to notice that their shrouds were in need of repair.

They were now by the northwest corner of the Church, and at a sign from the tall ghost they all followed him and marched around back to the Lawrence tomb. This was thrown open like a door in the solid masonry, and they began to descend in couples, such a crowd that they looked like mist, and no one stood out a distinct individuality in the transit.

The good-natured ghost then took the newspaper man by the arm and they followed the rest. No one took the slightest notice of them for which the man not yet dead was very thankful. He did not half like the idea of going down into the bowels of the earth among all these ghosts. As soon as they were down the young man saw to his surprise that there was a room so vast that his sight could not penetrate it to the end of it nor the width in any direction. It was lighted with a radiance so suave and pure that he wondered from whence it came.

The vast place was sustained by many columns of the finest marble, and was arched somewhat after the fashion of the church above. He could not repress an exclamation of surprise and pleasure, for never in his life did he see anything approaching it for beauty. Every column was carved in a different manner, and it seemed to him as if all the artists in the world or that ever lived had each made one, and this in competition with the others. One would be covered with flowers of such delicacy and perfection that it was impossible to believe them of marble, and the young man put out his hand and touched some of them to make sure that they were not some new and colorless plants growing down here. Others were covered with the most intricate designs, and the eye wearied in trying to follow the lines, so interlaced and complicated they were.

Others looked like lace. The fine lace pattern could be traced in all its daintiness, and it was a marvel of skill. Some of the columns resembled the tracery on the walls of the Alhambra, and some had vines through which peeped women's faces in all moods, ages and degrees of beauty. Twin columns stood in one place and, on these nothing but children's faces. Some of the babies carved on them were laughing, others crying, and so crowded, one beside another, and one above another that one wondered how so many could have been found in the world. Some of the babies were dead, others sick, some asleep, some plump and dimpled and more wan and wasted. Babies, babies, and yet more babies. The newspaper man was lost in astonishment at the number of them and the exquisiteness of the artist's work. He examined so many of these beautiful columns that his brain was weary with the effort.

Then he turned his gaze to the lighting of this immense place, and was surprised that he had not noticed it at first. There were arches innumerable, and each one of these was covered with glowing vines, all such as bear flowers. In some places were hung baskets of the most gorgeous orchids, with their pendant foliage. Many of the columns had passion vines covered with their mysterious blossoms. There were roses and clematis and hundreds of other flowers that he had never seen, all climbing up those arches, and drooping in graceful festoons. He suddenly became aware that all the light emanated from the flowers and the leaves of these climbing plants. The passion flowers emitted light of the natural color of these blossoms, and the roses shed soft radiance. Even the leaves and tendrils were incandescent. Every bud and flower gave its share of light and the effect of all these together was one of marvelous richness, yet it was delicate and beautiful beyond description.

The odor of the different flowers hung on the air until it was almost oppressive, but yet so delicious. The young man thought what a success this kind of lighting and decoration would be for some of the smart set who are always trying to find something new with which to surprise their guests. He made a mental note of it and said to himself that other men had become leaders in the domains of swelldom on less than this, and he decided to keep his eyes open for any other novelty which could be transplanted above ground.

There was a breeze from somewhere, and he saw that the festoons of incandescent flowers were swaying in the wind, and the movement set free hundreds of delicious odors until now unsuspected. He was trying to study out a plan by which the danger of fire could be avoided, and still preserve all the marvelous effect of the illumination. As he stood lost in his admiration he became aware that a man was watching him. As he turned the man made a ceremonious bow and said:

"Excuse me, sir; but may I ask if you are really as much interested in the decorations as you appear to be?"

"I certainly am," answered the young man, "and I wonder who could have done it. It must have taken many minds and many hands to have accomplished it. I am filled with wonder at the master mind that conceived it. Can you tell me anything about it?"

"Yes, for the original idea was mine, though many hands helped in carrying out the details. While I was alive, being a man of wealth and leisure, I amused myself in getting up unique affairs intended to amuse Society. I planned many things, both of a public and private nature, and if you will look over the files of the society papers of my time you will see that all were successful, even when I had but earthly hands and intelligence to depend upon. Our insight is keener now and our hands are no longer the clumsy things of life. Here I have but to formulate an idea and the artists, electricians and florists know my exact meaning; I flatter myself that the decorations here tonight are pretty fine. I do not believe that anyone could surpass them. What do you think?"

"I think it is marvelous. But, please tell me—am I not speaking to the great—"

"Hush, young man. No one is great or small here. Only some have more power than others for certain reasons. I undertook the getting up of this affair just to keep my hand in. I hope that when I get my passport I may be able to run things in the next sphere as I did in my own circle while I was alive."

The young man did not know exactly how to talk to the great man and so waited in silence for him to take up the conversation again. He did this by asking if the young man had noted many expressions of regret in the newspapers at the time of his demise.

The young man took note of the word demise and decided that somehow it sounded better than the less subdued one of Death, in a general way, and he thought it would sound so much better down here that he should make use of it. So he looked sympathetically at the ghost, who stood expectantly waiting, and said that he had been in school at the time, but he remembered perfectly well, and he had also heard the principal of the school tell the scholars about the demise of so famous a man, and one so useful. That his example was a noble one for the rising generation. While he was trying to think of something else to say, the ghost suddenly and very irrelevantly said:

"My dear sir, what do you consider the most satisfactory word in the English language?"

The young man blushed and stammered lamely that he did not exactly know, but would be glad if the shade of such an authority would enlighten him.

The great man pushed out his chest, and said pompously:

"I should say it is, satisfaction. I think there is no other word so strong in point of expressing a meaning to my mind. Now, I can say that I am in a state of complete satisfaction so far as the success of the origination of this fete is concerned. I have arranged so many other affairs out of doors that I was glad to try my hand in a new field. It has resulted in perfect satisfaction."

Here he paused to allow the young listener to signify that he fully concurred in the statement. The ghost passed his skeleton hand across his chin and in a philosophical manner continued:

"Life is full of unsatisfied ambitions and general unrest of mind, and hunger for food or power that nothing can satisfy but the actual realization and final satisfaction of all longings. There is another satisfaction, and that is realized revenge. When I came down here and left all the vanities and pomp of the world behind me, I heard that a certain society woman who had often tried to rebel and set aside my authority, and sometimes did really annoy me very much and interfered with my plans to a most unreasonable extent, said that now that I was gone Society could draw a long breath and call its soul its own. This woman prided herself on her fine presence. She even boasted that Death itself could not make her ugly or less imposing. I saw her a few minutes ago, and I honestly think she makes the worst-looking ghost I ever saw. I assure you that was a great satisfaction. But, to return to the decorations here. I would ask, have you seen the card room?"

"Card room! I was always led to think cards the invention of the Evil one, and I certainly never expected to find them here."

"My dear sir; you are behind the age. Cards are not by any means wicked in themselves, nor is it wicked to play them. The whole 600 play cards. Some of their card parties are among the most interesting functions down here. If Tom, Dick or Harry sit around in common places and play stud poker for the drinks, that is one thing. If Mrs. Schuyler Van Astorbilt has a card party, why it is all right to play poker, euchre or bridge whist, and if some lose why the others must win. They all are able to lose without depriving their families of bread. Therefore it is no sin for Society to play cards. I have decided that bridge whist is not worse than casino. There has been a lot of rot talked about the smart set, but not half of it is true—ah, yes; in a minute!"

This last was said by the man who had been talking with the reporter to a man who appeared to be quite excited about something. They talked for a few minutes in whispers, and then the newcomer, satisfied, went away, and the social leader and planner of the fete returned to the newspaper man with an apology, and said:

"You saw me just now? Well, that man came to tell me that there is a professional gambler in the card room. I must go and put him out. It would never do to let a professional gambler associate with our set. Many of them are here. Will you come with me?"

CHAPTER III
THE GAMBLER'S PENANCE

AS THEY WENT TOWARD the card room, the organizer of the banquet said: "You must not be surprised if I have to employ force to get him out, for he must go whether he wants to or not. It would never do in the world to allow the morals of our place to become contaminated by the presence of such creatures, so come on."

As they neared the card room they heard female voices raised in entreaty, saying: "Oh, Mr. Edwards, please do show us. We are at the mercy of all the society people and they put on such airs. We do not know how to play poker, and they cannot see what kind of training we have had. If you do refuse we shall never be happy, for we shall be forever shut out of good society."

Much more and in many different voices was said, until it seemed that the person to whom the appeals were made consented. Then there was a chorus of thanks. By this time the leader of the smart set and the newspaper man were in the room.

They stood and gazed at the scene before them. There were tables all around the room. Players were seated at nearly all of them. The young man noted that some played whist, others preferred euchre, while still others played seven-up and beggar-my-neighbor and other old and innocuous games, but many were playing poker. The cards were all right but there was a total absence of chips or money. All the betting was done with pebbles. The players were totally oblivious to everything going on around them.

The professional gambler was pointed out to the director of the ceremonies and he stood a little while looking at the man he was to put out. He was by all odds the biggest ghost there. His shoulders were broad and his arms long and massive. The leader stood thinking whether it would be quite safe to argue with him. He had always been a man of peace, and the only battles he had ever fought were those pertaining to matters of dispute in the social ranks above ground. He had been peacemaker there so often that he sometimes wondered that they had not killed each other off like Kilkenny cats. So he watched the gambler, and waited until he should do something which he might claim to be against the rules governing the conduct of affairs in this card room.

One or two of the oldest whist players came to him and endeavored to convince him that it was his duty to interfere before the professional gambler had contaminated the minds of the lady ghosts by his presence. These ladies were preparing to learn to play poker. But each time that he looked at the giant proportions of this ghost the leader felt that it was not his business to interfere. If they wanted to learn what did it matter to him? Finally, at the urgent requests of the others, he plucked up courage and strode over to Edwards with all the superhuman dignity of a hopelessly small man, and with an air that admitted of no discussion, said:

"Sir; I hear that you are a professional gambler. If that is so I must request you to retire from the presence of these ladies. This is a very exclusive part of the underground world—"

"Are you St. Peter?" asked Edwards, quietly.

"No: but I have been requested to see that nobody of questionable antecedents is admitted, as it is intended for the best class—I hope you will go quietly. There are ladies present and I do not wish to proceed to extreme measures. Otherwise I shall be obliged to put you out."

"Did you say that to me?" asked Edwards with ominous politeness. "For, if you did, I have this to reply. I am not in the habit of taking orders from anyone. But, if you still desire to try, I advise your friends to bring a basket. For, if you lay a hand on me there won't be a bone of you left big enough to make a toothpick of. Now, run along, little man and don't bother me. I am at the service of these ladies, and don't you forget it."

Saying this the big ghost of Edwards turned his back on the pompous little man, giving his undivided attention to the ladies who had asked him to teach them the noble and elevating game of poker. After one more comprehensive glance at the massive proportions of the man before him, the leader concluded that discretion was the better part of valor. He scarcely saw how he could back down from the position he had taken without a loss of dignity. His distress was so evident that the newspaper man felt really sorry for him. He knew that this man held a high position in the esteem of the ghosts and wished to help him. So he came to his rescue in this way:

"I do not think he will do much harm, and if a sort of private watch is kept on him, why, then, if he does anything offensive to good taste it will be time to act. If you are willing I will stay here and if anything is wrong I can report to you. What do you think?"

"So well of it that I will at once retire to the smoking room at the right of the entrance, and there you will find me if anything objectionable occurs."

Saying this the little great man went out and the reporter prepared himself to be amused beyond anything he had ever felt. He even expected to get more fun out of the affair than Edwards himself.

There were six lady ghosts, and they crowded around the big gambler endeavoring to console him for the unpleasantness that had just occurred. All, with one accord agreed that the society leader would do well to mind his own business. He was well enough to plan the banquet and get up the decorations but when he undertook to spy on them and dictate what they should do, they wanted him to understand that they were not of the wonderful 400 and didn't want to be. They thought themselves too good, so there!

The six ladies then took seats at one of the tables.

One might think that these six ghosts might look exactly alike, but not so, for every one had as distinct a personality as though she had not been dead so long that nothing remained but bones. But there was a sort of emanation of some indefinable kind; an atmosphere of some occult property that took the place of flesh and body. In some curious and inexplicable way this gave to each skeleton a separate individuality. Even the lay mind could understand this, and the newspaper man could tell the ghosts apart perfectly well.

One of these women was very small, and was clearly as pugnacious as a sparrow and as tenacious as one. The next one was a woman of the stately kind. The third was quite an old one, judging by her teeth, and sitting beside her was one with such beautiful teeth as he had never seen but once, and the sight quite unnerved him, too, for they belonged to the young girl whose wedding had brought him to this strange carnival of ghosts. The sight gave him an agonizing wrench of pain. He wondered how long it would be before she would be like these women, with nothing left of her sweet young beauty but her white and even teeth.

This ghost had a way of holding her head to one side and raising her hollow eyeless sockets in what was once a most effective attitude, but it was now but the travesty of itself. The sight filled the young man with deep pity. This ghost was a widow.

The fourth was as tall and angular as any of the two men ghosts without one redeeming trait. She was an old maid. It was easy for the young man to know all these things for some new and occult quality in his nature hitherto unknown gave him a new insight into the personality of the ghost and he saw them as they must have been in life, yet saw them only as ghosts. He sensed these things without knowing how he did so.

The old maid ghost told the widow that she had heard that Edwards had been a sad dog in his day, and that gave him added interest, for it must be admitted that women do admire sad dogs.

When they were all seated they waited for their teacher to make a beginning. He squared his shoulders, and tried to put his hands in his pockets when he was suddenly brought to a realizing sense that there are no pockets in shrouds. He also began to realize that he had undertaken a greater task than he had thought. He had no money nor chips, and so could not play poker. He looked the picture of misery.

He was thinking how he could get out of the place decently.

It was the practical old maid who suggested that they should play with beans. She had heard that that was sometimes done. Edwards stifled a groan.

When all the other women said that it was impossible to find beans, and that it would be better to use pebbles as the others were doing, the old maid told them to wait a moment, and almost before they missed her she was back with at least a peck of beans of different colors tied up in her shroud.

She tripped along in such a funny, affected manner that the newspaper man could not help smiling, though of course he hid that fact. For Edwards was a much larger man than he was, and he thought that a blow from one of those bony fists would make a ghost of him too. And he was not hankering after immortality just then.

The old maid emptied out all the beans, and they sorted the different colors into different piles. Edwards counted them and divided them all around into equal parts. Then he produced the cards and said: "We must have something to represent money and these beans—"

"Oh!" cried the sparrow ghost, "we must not bet. It is wicked to bet."

"Then you cannot learn to play poker," replied he.

"I don't see why," responded she pugnaciously.

"All right. Have it your own way. You will have to give up your poker lesson right now, for the betting is all there is to it."

There was a whole chorus of exclamation from the rest. The old maid ghost said that after so much trouble had been taken, and as none of the rest had any scruples against betting beans, she did not see why the rest could not go on, and Mrs. Fogg stay out. The big gambler waited with what patience he could muster, for the game had little zest to him without money.

He put the pack of cards back somewhere in his shroud and waited. On seeing this the other five took an anxious cry that he must not desert them. Quiet was restored on the promise that the betting with the beans should be regarded solely in a Pickwickian sense. So the beans were distributed. The black beans stood for fifty cents each, and the white ones for a dollar each, and the big red ones for five dollars.

"That is high enough for beginners, isn't it?" asked the old lady benignly.

The big professional gambler took a severe fit of coughing and shook so hard that the newspaper man thought surely he would fall in pieces, but he rallied and said:

"Now, ladies, I deal you each five cards. Your object will be to see how many of a kind you can get together."

"What kind?" asked the sparrow woman.

"Why, two aces, or three deuces, trays, fours or face cards all the way up. Aces are the highest."

"Which one?" asked the little woman.

"Higher than a ten?" asked the widow.

"I said the ace is the highest card in the pack," replied he.

"That is not answering the question, sir. I wish to know which one."

"Oh, any one," answered the man wearily.

"But I can't see how four aces can all be the highest," said the sparrow.

"I mean that they all count higher than any other card. After ace comes king, then queen, then jack, then ten and so on. Four aces make the best hand except a royal flush or straight. Two of a kind are good, three better, four best. I will explain the rest as we go along. Now I deal you each five cards—"

"You said that before," remarked one of the ghosts.

"So I did. Now you must decide upon your limit."

"I have five cards. I thought you said that was the limit," said she of the pretty teeth.

"I mean, how much do you want to bet? As you are beginners, suppose you make it a half a dollar."

"You said there was to be no betting," cried Mrs. Fogg, at the same time trying to match a pair of a jack of diamonds and a four of spades that she had spread out on the table before her.

"Oh, you each are to put a black bean on the middle of the table, and, madam, please never show your cards until you are called."

"Sir!"

"Oh," groaned the gambler, "what I mean is this. I will explain as we go along when someone calls for you to show down, but it is or should be your object to hide your hands—cards—as completely as possible from all the others."

"I don't see how I am going to find out if I don't look," grumbled the little woman.

The newspaper man was enjoying this mightily, and from time to time he cast pitying eyes at the unfortunate big ghost, for once he had had the pleasure of teaching three women to play the noble game, and he fully sympathized with the suffering man.

The ghostly gambler gathered himself together and said:

"Now, ladies; there are a number of complications in this game, and as they arise I will explain them."

"I would prefer to know them all at once," said she of the pretty teeth. "I am sure that I could remember."

The poor man began to look as if he thought that this was a job put up against his peace of mind, but he courageously continued:

"As I said, your object is to get as many pairs or cards of the same number of spots into your hand as possible, and if you have two pairs, or only one pair, you can draw three cards from the pack putting as many of those as you hold in your hand back—discard, they call that—and try and make up a full hand that way. Now each of you has five cards. Please look at them, and, well, as this is the first, perhaps it would be better for you to show them, and I will advise you what to do."

"You just told me not to show mine."

"Now, wouldn't that come and fetch you?" muttered the wretch under his breath.

"What's trump?" asked she whose teeth were so pretty.

The old maid scored a hit by putting her cards, hand and all, into the big paw of the gambler, and letting it lie there innocently.

"I'll scrape the pot," cried the old lady ghost, at the same time triumphantly showing two deuces and three trays.

"I—I—beg your pardon?" said the bewildered man.

"Isn't that what you say when you get better than anyone?" she asked defiantly.

"Oh, yes," murmured he faintly; "but we must wait and see what the others have got."

One lady had two queens, two jacks and a tray, and another had four fives and an ace. Mrs. Fogg had a four, a seven, a jack and two nines. She was highly indignant when she discovered that her hand did not count beside the others.

"If there is going to be such favoritism shown, I don't care to play," she said, pouting.

The woman with the pretty teeth had a pair of aces and three kings, and the old maid had a royal flush. It was a task beside which that of Hercules sunk into ignoble insignificance to explain just why a royal flush was higher than the pairs on which he had just laid such stress, while he had not even mentioned the royal flush at all. He made up his mind that he would not mention a straight even if one turned up every hand. The miserable man was nearly exhausted before they all understood, and he never thought of looking at his own hand at all. The chair where he sat was one of those old-fashioned kind, made of horsehair, and he kept slipping down, and by his gyrations alone anyone could have seen his uneasiness.

Finally, after much explanation they got down to a real game. Each got her cards, examined them defiantly and every one bet with a recklessness that had no limit but the amount of beans on hand. The last bean was on the table. After about forty-five different attempts, each prefaced and followed by explanations from the miserable ghost they had drawn and discarded.

"I did not need anything more," said the old lady, "but I thought I might get something better than four aces, so now I will stand squat."

"I—I beg your pardon?" gasped he.

"That is what you said, isn't it, Lavinia? I mean when you have all you want."

"Oh, pat, madam. I said pat."

"If you had meant pat, why did you say squat? Was it meant to confuse me?"

"What is trump, please," said the widow plaintively.

"There is no trump in poker, madam," said Edwards for the twentieth time.

The old maid leaned over and whispered confidentially:

"Please, dear Mr. Edwards; is mine a good hand?"

"I only wish that I might always be sure of holding one as good. Why, madam, it is simply gorgeous—a regular beauty."

"Oh, Mr. Edwards! You naughty man!"

"I see everyone and I make it five hundred better and I call," cried Mrs. Fogg, piling all her beans in a heap and then preparing one end of her shroud to hold her winnings. The big gambler had somehow found a pocketknife and this he jabbed surreptitiously into the chair as a relief to his feelings, while the six women were quarreling over the beans. They appealed to him, and the old lady said:

"Mr. Edwards, Mrs. Robinson hasn't anted at all for three hands, and Miss Shookes puts a handful of beans of all colors in the pot every time without counting them."

"Oh, well; she knows that this is only to learn. She wouldn't do that if it were real money."

"No, indeed; for I was always noted for my prudence about money. That is how I died richer than some folks I know of, who had scarcely enough to pay for their funerals."

"I think, ladies, that you could all show your hands now."

Mrs. Fogg triumphantly put six cards on the table. She had kept one of her discards to make up three pairs. This caused much animated discussion, particularly as Mrs. Washner had four fives.

"You said you had four aces," whimpered Mrs. Fogg when the case was decided against her.

"I did not, did I, Mr. Edwards?"

"I don't remember," replied he, wishing that he had had sense enough to go into the billiard room and stay there instead of making such an idiot of himself.

"I simply said that I drew that card to see if I could get anything better than four aces. Now, isn't that what you would call a bluff?"

"Yes; and it was a good one, too," said he admiringly.

"Besides Mrs. Fogg had six cards, and—"

"Well she didn't have the four aces, and that isn't half as honest as my having six cards. You told me, and you know it very well, that I was to get as many pairs as I could. She didn't have the aces, and I did have three pairs, and I am entitled to the beans, so now!"

The woman with the fine teeth looked dreamily at the gambler and silently laid down her hand. There were four aces and a king. None of the others had anything to beat this, and she smiled bewitchingly at him as he awarded her the beans, whereat Mrs. Fogg flew into a violent passion and sobbed tearlessly, until the poor man did not know what to do. She continued until he was ready to throw up the whole affair and leave as she said:

"I just don't care! I am sure Mr. Edwards just picked those cards out on purpose for her. I don't want the old beans. I detest beans, only I believe in standing up for principle, and I know that gamblers—professional gamblers—do cheat at cards."

"I think that a gambler—even a professional gambler—would have to be very unprincipled to try to win with six cards when he knew that that was the worst kind of cheating," said the old maid, taking up the man's defense with such an air of having the right to champion his cause that his jaw dropped and he made a movement as if for flight. At this point quite a number of other ghosts who had gathered around them began to clap their hands, and one said:

"Go in, little woman, and win. You will make a famous player in time."

The little belligerent hurriedly arose and said angrily:

"If Mr. Fogg were only here, you would see what would happen. I won't stay here to be abused. I was lowering myself anyway."

"I think so, too," said the old maid, "but it was by the way you have acted and not from your association with anyone here. We can spare you without sorrow."

By this time several more had gathered, and the ladies, seeing that they were attracting more attention than they desired, left the card room so sud-

denly that the newspaper man could not tell which way they went. Then he
looked for the big ghost. He, too, had disappeared. So the reporter, left to
himself, decided to go and find the leader and tell him the outcome of the
affair.

The young man thought that it might be that this affair was a form of
punishment for former sins of omission or commission. But he must indeed
have been a very bad man to deserve such a punishment as this, and he
thought, too, that no other form of punishment could have been devised so
well calculated to break a real gambler's heart. He felt sorry for him.

The reporter then went to the billiard room in search of the leader of the
evening's ceremonies. He was nowhere to be seen, and the young man stood
watching the billiard players. He thought they all seemed to be playing in
a perfunctory way, and there was no spirit in their play. Spectators stood
about watching the progress of the games, and occasionally making remarks
of approbation or derision.

There were several men there whom the young man felt sure he had seen in
life, but as none spoke to him he did not exactly like to press the acquaintance.
One of the men that he felt so positive that he had known in life had been
a rabid billiard player, and he neglected his family to such an extent that
the young reporter's mother once said that she hoped that when he died he
would have to play billiards continually for a few millions of years as a just
punishment. He was one of those who did not seem to be having a good time
at all.

Thinking that there might be things of more interest going on in other parts
of the place, the young newspaper man went out to the main hall. There were
things to see there.

CHAPTER IV
THE MENDED GHOST

JUST AS THE REPORTER was going out of the room he noticed a man hobbling along in the most painful manner. The upper portion of his body was of enormous proportions. Even the big gambler would have appeared dwarfed beside this man. But, large as he was, he seemed somehow to be unaccountably dwarfed, and the commendable curiosity belonging to newspaper men caused him to try and discover the meaning of this state of affairs.

As the man came hobbling along he tripped and would have fallen had not the young man caught him in his arms and held him up. The young man sustained him to a seat, and as he sank down in it he asked the ghost if there was anything else he could do, or be of any further assistance. The man, with the remarkable frankness that seemed to be a part and parcel of everything down here, replied:

"No, nobody can't do nothing for me. It was all done when I was moved. And it was done up good and brown too. Nobody can't now make my legs whole again; no, not if they tried forever and forever. It is a shame, that is just what it is!"

"Would you mind telling me what it is that has happened to you? I am sure it must be something unusual, and if I can help you I need not say how gladly I would try."

"No; you can't help me, nor nobody else can't. But if you like I will tell you about it and maybe someone else may be spared if you put a piece in the paper about it."

This caused the reporter to break out in a cold sweat, for he now felt almost afraid to think. The ghost resumed:

"I don't believe that nobody cares about us when we are once dead. I died and was buried in a vault under the old church that stands somewhere in Amity Street or close by. It may be gone now for all I know, for I haven't been there for a long time, and I don't care if the old shebang is torn down, for it is to that that I owe my misery. Just look at me! I was a giant in my life, and stood seven feet in my stockings and was big according. But, when my time came I was sick and died like the weakest critter of them all. My folks paid the seven dollars to have me put into the receiving vault like the rest. I was pretty comfortable for the first year. The rule was that when new corpuses came in they must be put into the receiving vault the first year. Afterwards they were put into the back vault to make room for the new comers. There was shelves in the first one, and nobody couldn't crowd his neighbors, but in the back vault he was laid just one coffin on top of another, and nothing between them. At one time there was over five thousand corpuses under the church, but hardly anybody knew it.

"The most of the coffins was old what was in the back vault, specially the lower line, and often when a new fellow was put in on top of the other lot the old coffins would mash down to nothing, and nothing of the body would be left, but the bones, and you can just guess how that squeezed. They kept on piling more and more until even with the crumbling old coffins there was no more room. Then the trustees or whoever it was that had the say, decided that we must all be moved to York Bay, and they set about moving us."

The reporter was deeply interested in this, and followed every word with the greatest care, for if it turned out to be true after he should be in a position to verify it, he intended to write it up for the benefit of humanity. The ghost accepted the chair which the young man brought him and continued his story.

"Them trustees thought that the sooner the job was done and the quieter they was about it the better it would be, and there was a whole bunch of fellows come to do it. They busted all the coffins what wasn't already busted, and they threw them into one heap, tore out all the linings, and took off the shrouds, that was left, and they threw them into one heap to sell for old rags. And all the plates and handles was took along with the rest. Then they brought a lot of common pine boxes. All the corpuses what wasn't claimed by the folks related to the corpus was just chucked into them, sometimes three and more in one. When they got three or four into one box and the lid wouldn't shut, they jumped on the top or jammed the bones down till it did. One woman had all her ribs broken and several others had their breastbones stove in to get enough of them into one box. There was one box fixed for three, and they chucked me in that head foremost. There was not half room enough, so my legs stuck out over two feet, and to make me fit in what did them dumb fools do but take a spade and just naturally chop off my feet right in the middle of the legs, and threw them in, and that is how I am in this fix. I tied them up the best I could, but to get a purchase I had to lap them as you see. They don't feel solid. I expect to fall down every step I take. See how I had to fix them."

As he said this, the poor giant, shorn not of his strength but of his length, stuck out his offending feet. Surely enough they were chopped off as he said, for the marks of the sharp spade were still visible. The two ends of the bones to each leg had been, as he said, spliced by sliding them past each other and then tying them in place. They lapped at least twelve inches and that cut the man's stature down two whole feet. The worst feature about it was that the parts were not, and could not be made solid enough to make locomotion safe or comfortable.

"If ever I get out of here alive," thought the reporter, "I shall make it impossible for folks to kick me around like that. I shall have it fixed so that my body will be cremated and the ashes hidden so that nobody can ever find them. Then he spoke:

"Your case is certainly a hard one, and I am surprised that the board of health ever allowed such things. Surely they must have known of it."

"Do you know, that affair was just the cause of the law that was passed making it necessary to have a Coroner's inquest on every body, and all the things that them fellows had piled up to sell was took away and burnt. The Police Gazette took and printed pictures about it, and that is the first time that I remember of seeing big headlines, and they was all about 'the awful desecration of the dead,' and the trusteeses had to do a lot of things to keep the people from making a fuss. After that they was a little more careful what they done to the bodies, but it was too late to do anything for me. This here affair was in about 1830, but I am not sure to a day about the date, for naturally we don't care so much about time when we are facing something else."

"Suppose I get you a pair of crutches?" said the young man with deep sympathy. The ghost said they could do no good, but that he was grateful that there was someone who showed a little feeling for one so long dead. He added that he hoped to get his release soon, as he had always been as good a man as he knew how to be, and when he did get his passport he would not need legs.

Almost as soon as he had said this the poor ghost sat back in his chair and went to sleep. After several vain attempts to rouse him the young man wandered around a little. He found that while he had been in the card and billiard rooms the tables for the banquet had been prepared, and he looked around in surprised admiration.

Each table was more than a hundred feet long, and there were so many of them that he soon gave up the attempt to count them all. The covers set on each table were seventy-five on each side with a seat of honor at the head.

The table service was something wonderful. It recalled a day when he went to see the preparations for a grand banquet at the home of the late W. H. Vanderbilt. All along three sides of the large dining room there were glass cabinets reaching to the ceiling, and in these there were great silver plates, and platters, side dishes, tureens, punch bowls, tankards, pitchers and goblets of every description, each a perfect work of art after its kind.

There were golden dishes of many shapes, all richly wrought and not one among them that was not worthy a close study for the beauty of form and fine goldsmith's work. But not all of that mass of gold and silver put together could balance the value and workmanship upon even one of the articles which stood so thickly on these tables.

Great pitchers of gold in the most exquisite rehausse and repousse work, filled to the brim with wine, stood all along the center of the tables, and around each were clustered golden goblets, according to the number of guests expected to be seated there. There were buffets in every direction, and quite a number of men had apparently found them already.

Upon the tables were all the delicacies that one could have found at the most perfectly appointed hotels. One table reminded the reporter of a grand ball and house warming at the home of the late Ogden Goelet, where there was not a piece of plate that was not duplicated here. Even the napery looked the same and set the newspaper man to wondering whether the ghosts did not borrow their plate and other things from the owners for the occasion.

Above, the festoons of the incandescent lights in the form of flowers shed their soft radiance, and also such perfume as would naturally exhale from such blossoms. All was a pleasure to the eye and taste.

While the young man was standing at the head of the central table there came the sound of a silvery note of music, such as might come from some sort of a horn, but wonderfully sweet and clear. It appeared that this was the signal for all the ghosts to take their places at the table. In an amazingly short time they were seated.

The reporter found that he had not been included in the list of the guests at the banquet. He felt a little vexed, though he really did not feel hungry, and he had an idea that he did not want to eat with the ghosts. He remembered a poem that he had read somewhere about ghosts drinking out of skulls newly torn from the grave, and he smiled at the contrast of these magnificent tables and viands.

The company was seated much as they would be at any other banquet, only there were no waiters. Everyone was seated and they all waited on themselves and each other, for, as he learned later the grave, like love, levels all things. And this in spite of the class distinctions mentioned before.

The ghosts were placed so that there was a lady and gentleman ghost side by side. The gentlemen were as punctiliously polite as could be desired and served the ladies with the greatest attention and assiduity.

At this juncture the Sociable Ghost came puffing up, much exercised, and said: "My dear sir, I beg you to pardon my apparent neglect, but the fact is there was a scrap between two famous old prize fighters, and you must excuse me if I forgot everything else for the moment. Why, for a time I really forgot that I was dead."

The young man murmured that he was quite excusable, and was about to disclaim any appetite, when the Sociable Ghost continued: "I say! It was fine! The old fellow put the kid to sleep in about ten minutes. We had a chance to learn more about good sparring than we ever knew before. I am sure that I could give an uppercut now such as was never known in my day.

"But, you really must join us. I had a seat reserved for you at this table where you can see everything that is going on, and where you will have a chance to learn many things of which you never heard. Ladies and gentlemen, permit me to introduce a friend of mine, who is not yet of us, but whom I have invited to pass the evening with us. I hope you will make him welcome for my sake until you learn to like him for his own."

There was a confused murmur intended as a welcome accompanied with bows from all the guests at this table. The newspaper man saw that all these ghosts were really hungry, and ate with genuine appetite. The wine was poured out in generous quantities, and they drank as if exceedingly thirsty, and soon the great hall rang with laughter, and lively sallies of wit and anecdote. He tried so hard to listen to them all that to his intense chagrin he found afterward that he could not remember half of it and what he did recollect was so disjointed that it was worse than none.

The ghost seemed to think it a great joke that one not dead should be among them, and many witticisms were launched at him on account of his too evident curiosity. The good-natured ghost told him that he probably would not get much nourishment out of what they gave him, and that he was very sorry that he could not offer him something to take home to the children, as was the custom when he was young. He told how he cried when his parents went anywhere and failed to bring him home some of the good things they had had at the party. The young man answered in the same strain and said that he was not hungry, and even if he were the feast of reason and flow of soul would more than satisfy him.

While the guests were eating, the young stranger within their gates was observing with great interest everything about him. There was quite as wide a difference in the way the ghosts acted as among the living, and he saw some shoveling the food into their fleshless jaws with knives. He remarked that some who ate with their knives tried to give something of grace to the movement by turning the blade outward, and these ghosts held their spoons with the points to the mouths and to render this more elegant they stuck one little finger out stiffly, while grasping the handle in their bony fingers.

One man poured his coffee into his saucer, when the great leader ventured to remind him that in polite society people drank their coffee from the cups, whereupon the offender asked him with some warmth if he set himself up to be better than George Washington, and assured him that the Father of his country poured his coffee and tea out into his saucer, and he suggested that the leader go back to his beautiful society, and see if they did not do things that no self-respecting ghost would do, or even dream of condescending to do. Then the other ghosts took it up and the feeling ran so high that it almost resulted in throwing the leader from the place. Then one peace-loving ghost stood up and said:

"My friends, it ill becomes us to quarrel over a matter of such little importance. Not all of us were born in the time of ultra-civilization. Most of us never saw a four-tined fork while alive, and so we were obliged to convey our food to our mouths with our knives. I do not believe it a capital sin. I well remember that I was once at a dinner where there were several clergymen and great men from various walks of life. This very gentleman's grandfather, who now objects to the use of a saucer, used a knife. I know, for in listening to something that was said he forgot and put it into his mouth. The sharp edge was toward his mouth and he cut his lip quite badly and made it bleed. Everybody used their knives then. Tea plates were considered part of every table service from the highest down, and they were set on the table to stand the cups in while the tea or coffee was in the saucer to cool before being drunk. It is good manners for half the world to eat with the fingers, and I cannot see how any person has a right to dictate what anyone shall or shall not do." The leader stood up and angrily said:

"Of what use is our boasted civilization if we are to live like the beasts of the field?"

"Some of us here doubtless wish that we had lived like the beasts of the field while they had the chance and failed to do so," replied the former speaker. "Honestly, sir; is there anything you can bring forward to prove that the 'beasts of the field' ever did anything wicked that you can bring against them now? If you do you are wiser than I, and I assure you that I would rather be the most wretched little yellow dog that I know of than be some of the men who hold such exaggerated opinions of their own importance. Such men should have several billions of years allotted to them in which to learn that they knew nothing worth knowing."

The leader was so angry that he simply could not find words to reply. He glared at the speaker with such haughty and malevolent disdain, that one might have thought that this was some great social function above ground and that he was squelching some upstart with nothing but his millions to recommend him. He stared until the old ghost who had been trying to act as moderator began to show symptoms of a disposition to arise in his might and wipe up the floor with the great little man, so he haughtily turned away.

As soon as this little diversion had passed off, the eating which had been suspended was now renewed with fervor. New beakers of wine were poured out, and drank with gusto. The noise of the fleshless jaws clapping together as they ate was like the patter of hailstones on the roof. It became so loud and insistent that the newspaper man grew so nervous that he could have screamed like a hysterical woman, but he set his teeth and kept quiet.

He desired to enter into conversation with some of the ghosts, as there were many questions—important ones still unanswered. To that end he addressed himself to the old lady who had been trying to learn poker. He asked her if she would have some more wine, but she said:

"No, I thank you, sir; but I should like some of that boned turkey. I always liked turkey, and folks that ever eat of my turkey—roast turkey—for that is how I think a turkey should always be cooked—not that some other ways aren't good for a change that is. I was called a good cook and housekeeper in my day, and it has been my worst trial to see the awful messes my family has had to put up with since I am gone. And, the awful waste, and the dirt in my house. I used to keep them all on pins and needles all the time for fear of dirt, or that a fly would be let in. I never gave one of them a minute's peace. I thought I was doing a notable thing, then, but since I have had time to think it over it has come to me that I might have been a little less exacting. If I had been perhaps my boys would have stayed with me, but they couldn't stand so much nagging. Well, my poor old husband has got the dyspepsia trying to eat such cooking as he has to put up with now. And down here I naturally don't have a chance to cook. I think I could feel reconciled to being dead if I could only cook a meal of victuals once in a while."

"I don't ever want to cook, and I'd go plumb crazy distracted if I had to," said another woman ghost. "I had to cook for my father, five brothers, and all the farm hands, and every one of them with different tastes, and none of them ever satisfied. I nearly died trying to please them all. I used to get so tired that I wanted to die long before I did. Then a man asked me to marry him, and I thought it would be easier to please one man alone than all the sixteen, and I took him. You ought to have seen the way my folks went on! You just ought to have seen it! You would think I had committed an unpardonable sin, but it was done and I must confess that I am glad at the way they have to live now. Father hired many housekeepers, one after another, and when he found one that could really cook he married her. As soon as she was mistress she wouldn't lift her hand to cook a meal, and my brothers all died. Some of them have told me when they saw me here that they were awful sorry, and wished they could undo it all. But, my husband was worse than all the others combined. I just couldn't tell all he made me suffer. At last I gave up and died in self-preservation. I died to get out of the eternal kitchen."

"Why, Martha," said another ghost, "I never knew it was so bad as that. I always thought you cooked because you liked it and was too proud of your faculty to ever let anyone take your place."

"Well, I didn't; but I hated worse than all that anyone should know how bad I did hate it. I reckon if we knew all that goes on in our neighbor's hearts we would have a little more charity. You used to say that I neglected my church duties, and didn't sew for the heathen, and many a tract you left me on the sin of idleness, me what had been up every morning for ten years at four o'clock, and never got to bed till ten and eleven, working every minute all the time. Sometimes I felt like telling you to mind your own business. It is all over now, but I should like to know how much good has all your sewing for the heathen done you towards getting your passport? As you know the truth now, Melissy, which would you rather be: the enlightened Christian with the responsibility of knowledge of good and evil, or the ignorant heathen?"

"Yes: I know now, Martha, but I did not then, and now, if it is not too late, I want to ask your forgiveness."

This last was said with an evident disposition on the part of "Melissy" to fall upon the bony neck of "Martha" that an unregenerate man said with a harsh, rasping laugh:

"Forget it, forget it! This is no time to bring up old scores. If it were so, there are several fellows here tonight that I could lick with a clear conscience. I don't hold enmity, but I will say that they will do well not to rouse the sleeping lion."

As this ghost spoke, he turned his face toward two men at a table a short distance away, and waited to see the effect of his words. As no one took up the challenge the man sat down again at the table.

The newspaper man looked at this ghost with considerable interest, and thought that of all the ghosts he was the cleanest. He had noticed this ghost sitting at a rude table near the door. There was a candle burning there and an inkstand, and two immense books. The ghost sat balancing a pen, but was doing no writing. He had noticed him then as his skull and bones fairly shone, so white and polished they were.

It was not the intention of the young man to ask any impertinent questions about anything he saw there, but he thought to himself that when he was alone with the good-natured ghost he would ask him how this phenomenon had occurred. While he was thinking this, a polished ghost turned to him and said:

"Young stranger, I notice that you are somewhat interested in me, and far from feeling hurt at your natural curiosity, I am flattered by it and if you wish it I will tell you in a few words how it happens that I am so white after having been so long dead."

The young man felt his blood all mount to his face as he saw that even his secret thought could not be hidden, and he reflected that if even these ghosts knew what he thought, how impossible it would be to hide action or thought from the Master, as the ghosts called the One.

"Ahem! young sir, that is the right feeling. But to resume. I was married to a very sensible and worthy woman, with no nonsense about her. She kept her house well, and everything that she could do for my comfort and happiness she did. I felt very badly to leave her, but once you are called you must go, and I went. At that time Long Island City was scarcely more than a hole in the ground, and the church to which I belonged found that it would soon become necessary to remove from New York City, so they purchased a plot of ground quite in the outskirts of the former named place. I was laid in the old churchyard until they should be ready to remove us all. We were finally taken over there and put into the meanest kind of ground, all soaked with tidewater and the refuse of ages, which had been swept there by the tides until it grew to what no one with any regard for the truth would call solid ground. It is unhealthy even for a dead man.

"Well, there was a sudden rush for that place for its commercial value, and if I remember rightly I laid about where the big sugar refinery now stands. But it may have been a little further along, for I had the chills so bad during all this time that it is not to be wondered at if I am a bit hazy as to the exact location. We were all glad when we were moved from that place to one further from the shore. This was really a comfortable graveyard, but somebody wanted this place, too, and we found that we had congratulated ourselves too soon, and we were informed that we were to be moved again.

"In those days the best coffins were made of solid mahogany, and the longer that remains in the ground the more solid it grows. Several years had passed, perhaps thirty, and when we were moved many of the cheaper coffins had crumbled to nothing. It was not an easy job to arrange for these bodies, for this removal was so long after the burial that there were no friends left to see to it, and the church had to bear the expenses, and we who are dead know what that means."

As the polished ghost said this, there was a long drawn sigh from the whole assemblage that set all the lights flickering. He continued, sadly and solemnly:

"I will not dwell on the inconvenience of that removal, though I was left out all night in the rain. Still no one was to blame for that. Some of those whose coffins were of poor wood got very wet and some of them have had rheumatism ever since. Ghostly rheumatism, you know.

"At last we were put into another cemetery in Williamsburg, another most unhealthy place for ghosts. None of us felt at home there. We began to expect another removal as this place was building up rapidly, and we used to talk it over and hope that when we were moved again we should be put so far out on the Island that no one would ever want the land.

"It came upon us after all like a shock when we heard that we were to move on again, like Jo in Bleak House. Whatever old coffin had held together before now fell apart. My coffin was of mahogany, but in the last removal somehow, half of the lid was knocked off, and one from some other coffin was put in its place. Naturally that did not last as long as my own cover, and so when the coffins were all laid out for the final removal I felt how very frail and rotten this one was, and was in great fear that some incautious movement would cause it to crumble. I do not know why it is that coffins have that faculty of crumbling away to dust. I never noticed any other wood that did it. However, all who had any living relatives were properly removed, but those who had none had to go the way of friendless ghosts, and there were things said and done that would have caused trouble had there been anyone capable of objecting.

"My wife came and insisted that my coffin should be opened, but it was against the rule, for the sexton who had care of the removals had taken extra care that all should be done so that there would be no difficulty in identifying the bodies in case of need. My coffin therefore was all right, save for the lid; but she would not accept it on that account unless she could be permitted to open it. That they would not do.

"She tried every way to get them to consent, but the Board of Health had made the law so, and what do you think she did? She sent the men off on an errand, and took a spade that was lying near and pried the lid off so that she could see me, and when the men came running back, she said: 'That's him. I would know his head anywhere, it was so long.' She was so glad that she had outwitted the authorities that she did not complain about the lid. But she was tired of moving me around, and so had me taken home where I had lived and died, and there she kept me all these years, 'just to have a man about the house' she said. As she was one of the cleanest women in the world, she could not bear to see the mold of the Long Island mud on me, and every

Saturday I had a bath. She put clean clothes on me, and always did as long as she lived. We both lie now at Kenisco. I hope there will be no removal from there, but you must not blame me if I have lost confidence when it comes to be a question of routing out the dead to make place for the living, if there is money in it."

CHAPTER V
THE PRINCESS FROM EGYPT

WHILE THE POLISHED GHOST was relating his varied experiences, the women were talking, and the young man found that his thoughts wandered as he noticed a couple of articulated skeletons. He wondered if their experience would not be worth an effort, and was trying to think up some plan by which he could get them to talk, but before he could do so a man, on the other side of the woman who hated cooking, said solemnly:

"Now, maybe your folks had dyspepsia. That excuses much, and some folks that are not really nagging by nature get so by their sufferings. Now, I knew a fellow, and he was something awful. Nobody couldn't do nothing to pacify him after he had had his dinner, and at last it got so that smoking injured his vitals and his victuals done him no good."

"Did he pine away and die slow or go off all of a sudden at the end, as it were?" asked the old lady sympathetically.

"Well, I disremember, for I was in California that year and when I came back he was gone."

The young reporter thought this was a good time to try to learn what death really meant, and so he chose out a ghost whose frontal development was such as to give the appearance of great intellectuality, and said modestly:

"Sir, I hope you will not take it amiss if I ask you a few questions—"

"Fire away!" replied the ghost.

This unexpected answer quite took his breath away, but he managed to keep a sober face and asked:

"I wish very much to know how a man feels when he knows that he is drawing his last breath, when in short, he knows he is dying. If it is not asking too much I should like to have as many of you as are willing to tell me, each his individual experience." One thoughtful-looking man waited a moment and as nobody else took up the question he said:

"I think few of us are conscious when the last moment comes. We have all probably been so ill that there was a complete blank, and where by accident or any mortal injury it stands to reason that the shock and hurt would render the person unconscious. You may not know that I was a bishop in my life time.

I thought that I had nothing to fear, and so as I lay ill—I suffered a long time with the gout—the usual result of eating and drinking—at last it went to the stomach and I died. Before departing, I called my weeping friends and told them that the Lord had called me and I was ready to go. I posed as a martyr and angel of grace, and my deathbed farewell was spoken of as edifying. I really believed I was almost a saint, and it was for a long time a matter of surprise to me to discover that I was not wafted to immediate glory. I had yet to learn that from him to whom much shall be given much shall be required. And here I am, the least among you all."

Another ghost took up the subject and said:

"The most of you here will think it queer, but when I was drawing my last breath I knew it, and my principal feeling was anger that now one of my neighbors would get my favorite horse. He had long tried to buy it, and I would not sell, but what could my widow do with that horse when I was dead? After that there was a few seconds of blank and I felt myself drawn out of my own body and in another moment I was standing looking at myself. It certainly was a strange experience, and I am glad it is all over.

"I have talked with many ghosts and they all agree that death itself is not so dreadful. It is like going from a light room into a dark one and no one knows what is there. I find that almost every one has felt the same fear of the unknown, but it is after all so small a change. Many have a feeling as if they were falling a great distance to a profound depth in the darkness, but so far I have never found one who was really afraid of dying. It was more like the thought of the plunge into an icy bath. Sickness and physical suffering have a tendency to deaden the senses. And death itself is not so much of a change as we are prone to regard it. The way I now look at it is that it is simply one of the systematic changes made from time to time, from one sphere of existence to another, according to the great eternal plan toward a better kind of man. I used to wonder if this creature here who ravages and eats everybody else, and who is altogether unworthy and vicious and selfish was the best there could be, but now that I have an inkling into the future existence, I believe that we are but atoms in one great plan, and as worlds have been formed in their perfection, so will man stand out at last as the finished being he is intended to be, in the right time as grain is ripened."

The bishop bowed his head in assent to this, and that set the reporter to thinking about the great agnostic Ingersoll. He asked the company at large if they could tell him if Col. Robert Ingersoll were present. The whole company waited for the bishop to answer this question as though he were the proper one to do so. He spoke at last; but as if he would have preferred to waive the question:

"No, Mr. Ingersoll is not here. He got his passport the same day he died."

"I—I—thought he believed—or didn't believe—I really do not know how to express it—" stammered the young man in his excitement.

"Young man," said the bishop impressively, "it is not what a man believes, or thinks he believes, while on earth, that gains heaven, but what he does."

All the ghosts clapped their hands and shouted, "Hear, hear." The young man found food for the thought in the fact just told him. He made a resolution to become acquainted with the words of the man who had received his passport the same day he died. And, moreover, he intended to follow them.

There was a ghost who up to now had taken no part in the conversation, and he suddenly fixed the newspaper man with a compelling glance and said, slowly and impressively:

"It seems to me that no one has exactly answered the question about the phenomenon of death, which is in reality no greater than that of birth. We see that, but even the wisest men of all time knows no more of the life principle than the most ignorant. We know only that we enter this world and quit it through the doors of pain. When my own final moment came, I knew it and braced myself so that if ever I should be able to tell those still of the world all the sensations I experienced I would do so. If this is my opportunity I am glad of it.

"In the first place, I was a strong man and nothing but the pneumonia ever seemed to get a hold on me. I was ill about a week, and they all thought I was getting better, and for that reason I refused to take any more medicine, though really that would have made no difference anyway, for my time had come.

"Suddenly I felt a strange sensation, as if someone were pouring cold water into my lungs, and in a few minutes—perhaps seconds—my lungs were full of water. I was drowning just as much as if I had fallen into the water. I held my breath for a moment, and when I attempted to breathe it was impossible to do so. I had a moment of dizziness, and after that I saw everything about me quite clearly, and I opened my eyes twice more. Then I felt that if I could only get the water out of my lungs I would be all right. With one last effort I turned over in bed and tried to let the water run out, but it was useless, and I said to myself that the only thing was to get out of my body, for I felt stifling and knew that if I did not breathe I should succumb. The struggle for breath continued and I suddenly let go and fell free from my body, and it was quite ten minutes before I realized that the relief I experienced was because I was dead. At least, so far as the life I had left was concerned.

"When I did realize it I think my principal sentiment was anger at myself for my foolishness in trying to get loose from my own body. Death means to my mind simply that the time allotted to you and your little needs in this universe has expired, and you must go to the next, which is this existence where we have not yet been purified of our earthly dross. I may add a few more words, though they are only thoughts of my own, based on what I have seen and been told. I believe that all women who die in motherhood, sailors who are drowned at sea, all who have lived pure and honest lives, all the oppressed of all peoples, all little children and many grown persons who never saw or even heard of a church, are in some way and for reasons beyond our understanding, given their passports at once. Perhaps the Master who knows the heart's innermost thoughts knows that—well—I can only say that I wish that all people know what our bishop has just said: 'It is not so much what a man believes as what he does that wins heaven for him.' "

At this moment a tall ghost arose at the end of the principal table, looked around with a pompous air and in the attitude of a Sunday-school superintendent, addressing the unfortunate children, said in a clear, strong voice:

"Ladies and gentlemen, we have gathered here tonight in accordance with our privilege and in the performance of our duty, and we have banqueted on the choicest viands."

Here one ghost was heard to mutter that he didn't give shucks for all their choicest viands, and he would prefer any day in the year a good dish of baked beans or bean soup to all their boned turkey and pâté de foie gras, and as for the highfalutin sweets he had rather have a mince or pumpkin pie." There were some gentle murmurs of approval at this declaration of faith, but the speaker turned severe eyes upon the grumblers, whereat they subsided. The tall ghost continued his speech:

"We will now propose a toast to the ladies, and I wish to include our guest of honor, the Princess Shep, from Egypt. This noble lady has left her sarcophagus at the Museum of Art for this occasion, and it is our desire that she be installed in the seat of honor at the head of this table and afterward at the end of the hall where she can see the dancing and hear the speeches, and also hear the epitaphs such as are put upon our graves. This lady has been dead over five thousand years, and has seen much in that time of which we are entirely ignorant. Permit me, ladies and gentlemen, to present the Princess Shep, to whose most marvelous state of preservation we must do honor."

At this point he led the Princess, who was greatly hampered by her windings to a chair much higher than the others, and seated her there with much ceremony, at the same time gallantly lifting one of the little brown hands to his grinning mouth.

As soon as she was seated the master of ceremonies rapped sharply for order, and then said:

"Ladies and gentlemen, we have several friends from Derby, Conn., and part of this evening's entertainment will consist of hearing them recite their remarkable epitaphs, and so allow me to introduce the ladies first. I have the honor of presenting Mrs. Desire Kimberly, relict of Mr. Israel Kimberly, who exchanged this life for immortality August 21st, 1794, age 28."

Saying this he took the hand of a small ghost, who arose to her feet, and stood bashfully, like a child at school examinations. The tall ghost said:

"Mrs. Kimberly will repeat her own epitaph, and I will say here that in spite of its length—its very unusual length—she has managed nearly half of it already."

The lady began in a strident voice and repeated the verses, while the reporter took surreptitious notes, holding his book under the table cloth, for he felt just a little delicate about letting them know he was among them taking notes, but on the other hand he knew that he could never remember anything that had dates, or verses. He desired to be absolutely correct about this epitaph, so he took down as she repeated:

"Sacred to the memory of Mrs. Desire Kimberly, who exchanged this life for immortality, August 21st, 1794, age 28."

As she said this one woman near the newspaper man said to the one on the other side that she thought it entirely unnecessary for her to go over all that rigmarole, as the gentleman had just said it. The other lady in blissful ignorance of this byplay continued with her epitaph. The rest was the poetry.

"Here she bids her friends adieu, Some angel calls her to the spheres; Our eyes the radiant saint pursue, Through liquid telescope of tears."

She sat down with murmurs of applause all around. The master of ceremonies took his stand again and said while he waved his hand:

"Ladies and gentlemen, this is Mrs. Betsy Pease, who departed this life May ye 8, 1797, in ye 21st year of her age. Mrs. Betsy Pease was the wife of Mr. Isaac Pease, daughter of Mr. Thaddeous Bald. Mrs. Pease, ladies and gentlemen."

The lady began her recital in a very sing-song voice:

"With pangs severe strangling in blood, She soon became a lifeless clod; The summons of her God she obeyed, She closes life and ends her days."

With a low courtesy, not altogether devoid of grace, she sat down, evidently as much pleased as an elocutionist after she has recited Curfew shall not ring tonight. The applause was fainter, but she appeared satisfied. The master of ceremonies again stood up to introduce Miss Mary Hunter, who died in 1782, aged 17. She arose to her feet, and as she did so she seemed to stretch out like the gates to a ferry boat until she reached her full height, which must have been at least six feet. She had a harsh, rasping voice, and in a slow and impressive manner she said:

"She is not here, 'tis but a veil of clay That molders into dust beneath this stone; Mary herself in realms of fadeless glory Has put a robe of fadeless glory on. This monumental urn is not designed To tell of beauties withering in the tomb, Her brightest charms were centered in her mind Which still prevail and will forever bloom. Her conscious soul Allied to angels hails the glorious change, And joins the blest societies above In all the freshness of immortal love. There is a world of bliss hereafter, else Why are the bad above, the good beneath The green grass of the grave?"

This whole performance was so irresistibly comical that the unfortunate young man had such a sudden fit of strangling that two of the most muscular ghosts smote him on the back until he was in danger of having his spinal column dislocated, while the beauteous Mary sat down with an air of pride, which was quite natural when one considered the difficulty under which she labored. As she sat down she seemed to double up like a jackknife or a two-foot rule. There were murmurs of commiseration over the length of this epitaph, and the reporter thought to himself that it was rather a queer idea to contrast the robes of fadeless glory with the few rotting remnants of her cerements.

Scarcely had she taken her seat when a woman stood up, and as if she feared she would not get a chance to recite her effusion, she began and rattled it off in one string without punctuation, though to be sure this seemed to be a common fault with these ladies. She said:

"Mary Jane Smith, died Feb. 1st, 1752, age 43. Affliction sore long time she bore, Physician's art was vain, Till God did please that death should seize And ease me of my pain. Farewell my husband and my children, Farewell to all on earth, I hope to meet you all in heaven, Where parting is no more."

Mrs. Smith's ghost sat down in the consciousness of having taken time by the forelock and that now she was sure that no one could defraud her of her chance to recite the atrocity which she seemed to think so worthy of admiration. The master of ceremonies was evidently put out to think that anyone should take liberties with his program, so that he grew rattled a little and instead of continuing to call upon the rest of the ladies he hurriedly said:

"If Mr. John Beers is here will he please rise and tell us what they put on his gravestone?"

A very decrepit old man stood up after several trials to do so and in a weak and quavering voice repeated:

"John Beers, a Revolutionary pensioner, died April 22, aged 45. He fell as falls the oak with years, Which storms have beat upon, Upon his grave we shed our tears, To heaven we hope he's gone."

As this feeble old man sat down it seemed to the young man that it was a little hard on the old man's memory that they had left his ultimate destination in doubt. Still, as the old man made no objection no one else had any right to complain. The old man received quite an ovation. As he subsided the master of ceremonies said:

"Is Mr. Peleg Eddy here? I am sorry to say that I have never had the pleasure of meeting Mr. Eddy, so I cannot tell which one of our invited guests he is."

He looked around three or four times, and again asked for the gentleman from out of town. Finally a gloomy-looking little man stood up with a very bad grace. He could not have been more than five feet tall in life and was now considerably less. He repeated:

"Peleg Eddy and his wife, They sat out in early life. They turned about each other's hearts, But God doth call and they must part. 'Tis hard to part and leave behind A tender wife and child so kind. With anxious care she watched his bed, And kept cold towels on his head, But all in vain, for God doth send And call away her bosom friend. To his dear mother standing by, Saying, 'Dear mother, prepare to die, The heavens in glory is full in view,' He soon did bid this world a long adieu. A few hours after his senses fled, And now he sleeps among the dead; Sleep on, sleep on, and take thy rest, God called thee home we all thought best."

As this unfortunate man, whose family had laid this heavy load on him, sat down there were murmurs of condolence all around, and the newspaper man asked if he would permit him to ask where he was buried, whereupon he glared in the most ferocious manner at the interloper, while his bony fists clenched ominously:

"You may ask if you like, but I shall not answer. Do you think it is not enough to have to lie under that stuff without letting all the rubberneckers in the country know where it is that they may come and make fun of it?"

The young man disclaimed any such intention, and said that he regretted having asked, and apologized so abjectly that at last the poor ghost unbent a little and volunteered the information that the widow who had been such a ministering angel with her cold towels had wedded again in just one year, "and his name is Whipple, and I am just laying for him. If ever I do find him I am going to pulverize him. He wrote that epitaph and my wife thought it such a wonderful poetic effusion that she lost her heart, and common sense. I wait year after year in hopes of meeting him. Have you any idea how many centuries it will take to rub out all that?"

The newspaper man told the unhappy ghost that there was no punishment too great for a man guilty of such a pack of doggerel, and he meant it, and made another mental note that he should leave strict orders that no epitaph should be put over his resting place when he should be no more. The master of ceremonies now stood up and announced:

"I have the honor to announce that Sergeant Benjamin Davis, who was in the Civil War in the Seventh Regiment of Connecticut Volunteers is here. He participated in sixteen battles and served four years. He will now speak."

The ghost of the young man stood up, and he wore the shreds of his uniform, and so was the only ghost who did not wear what was left of his shroud. He said modestly:

"Ben. F. Davis, a sergeant in the Seventh Connecticut Volunteers. Participated in sixteen battles with conspicuous bravery and contracted chronic—"

Here he was suddenly interrupted by the leader of society, who said with great concern:

"Sir, do not forget that there are ladies present."

"Who is this galoot? By what right do you assume, sir, that I was about to insult these ladies? It is a good job for you that there are ladies present. I would use you for a curry comb otherwise. Now, then, just you close the doors of your face, as Job says. I contracted chronic rheumatism and died of rheumatism of the heart. Have you any objections to make to that?"

"No, not at all, only it was probably heart failure, instead of what you say. It is not fashionable to have rheumatism of the heart now, for it is dignified as heart failure. We have heart failure, and appendicitis, and laryngitis—"

"Folks die of them just the same, don't they?"

"Yes: but it sounds so much more refined."

The soldier boy looked at the man whose refinements were so much greater than the occasion required from head to foot, and then said defiantly:

"I don't see that you make any better looking ghost than the rest of us, and for two cents I would smash that ugly skull of yours, or at least reduce that very evident bump of self-esteem."

At this juncture the master of ceremonies was struggling with an overwhelming desire to laugh, for no one liked this man who always felt it a bounden duty to find fault with everyone and everything. But, at last he managed to rap for order and when the other ghosts had ceased laughing at the leader's discomfiture, he said:

"Ladies and gentlemen, by some mischance I failed to see the name of a lady from Derby, one whom we should all delight to honor, and I now ask Mrs. Hannah Clark to rise and favor us with her epitaph. Mrs. Clark, ladies and gentlemen."

As he said this the old lady arose to her feet, and holding to the edge of the table repeated in a weak and quavering voice:

"Hannah Clark, died September, 1801, aged 91. Her lineal descendants at the time of her death were 333, viz.: 10 children, 62 grandchildren, 242 great-grandchildren and 19 great-great-grandchildren. During her long life her company was the delight of her numerous friends and acquaintances. Having performed the duties of life and being impressed with the reality and importance of religion she died as she had lived, satisfied and happy."

As she said these words there came a strange and subtle change over her seamed and wrinkled skull, and she seemed to be putting on some filmy veil that softened all the outlines of the bones, and she said in a voice that grew sweeter and stronger with every word:

"My dear friends, it is borne in upon me that my time has come to leave all that belongs to this stage of existence and go where my Master calls me. It has come very unexpectedly, for I had not hoped for my passport for many long years yet. Adieu, adieu!"

Even as she spoke she was undergoing a change that was so wonderful that the whole assemblage, including the reporter, watched her intently. First, the bones of her skeleton grew misty and indefinite, and in their places there gathered a soft, filmy, nebulous mass of floating particles, and little by little they united into a misty, floating body, and this in turn took the form of the dead woman's face before decay had touched it. The features were defined as those of a lovable old lady, and flesh appeared to clothe the fleshless bones.

For a moment she looked at the people, and then with a smile of ineffable sweetness she vanished into nothingness, the tender smile seeming to remain even after all the rest had vanished. For several minutes everything was still, with that strange stillness which sometimes falls upon a whole community, without apparent reason, when every sense is alert, though nothing tangible is seen. The young newspaper man felt a lump rise in his throat, and two tears jumped suddenly from his eyes and rolled unheeded down his cheeks as he thought of the years of toil this woman had borne without thought or hope of recompense, and now she was so signally blest. The sight laid one more stone in the foundation of the resolves made this night as to his future. That the occasion was a solemn one, the silence and evident awe of the other ghosts was proof. Besides, the fading face was so glorified, and wore such a beatific expression that no one who saw it could doubt the fact that her season of penance was ended.

Filled with these thoughts, and marveling at it all, the young man scarcely knew that all the tables had disappeared, when he found himself sitting alone on a chair in the middle of the immense room.

He hastily rose to his feet and started off to find the Sociable Ghost, but he was nowhere to be seen, and so he entered into a conversation with a man who had been sitting silently at the table, and asked him if he could tell him how such a transformation had taken place and what had become of the bones, or had he been the victim of an optical illusion? The man replied:

"No one knows the hour of his release until it comes, and when it does, all the bones and all other material parts fall into impalpable dust and go to help build more worlds. From now on the spirit is free from all hindrance, and it is to be supposed that it passes to a better sphere. That is all we know about it. We all hope for the hour of release, but only the Master can tell when we have earned the right."

Probably the man would have said more on the subject, had not the ghost of Peleg Eddy come along and stopped, saying angrily:

"Aha! I have found you at last! You are the idiot that wrote that epitaph to weigh me down forever! And, you married my widow—"

"You ought to pardon me the first on account of the last."

"You are a liar, sir—"

Peleg Eddy interrupted the conversation right here, for the other ghost doubled up his fist and let it go, and it went in the direction of Peleg's head, and that not being on very strong, owing to the fact that the bones were very small, the head rolled to the floor and on for some little distance, while there was a general shout of laughter at the mishap. Peleg ran after it and putting it under his arm for safety, said in trembling tones:

"You had better take care, sir, and not arouse the sleeping lion. Don't turn the tiger loose in me. I am afraid to say of what I am capable when I am aroused fully."

"Oh, don't be afraid to tell us, for nobody else is afraid, but I advise you to go and take a nap, and if in that sweet slumber you even dream that you can thrash me I shall know it, and I will give you one that will last you a thousand years. I owe you one for dying anyhow, or I should never have married your widow. She led me a dog's life, and I just feel like taking it out of you."

By this time all the ghosts were tired of a quarrel promising so little real fight, and they sauntered off in different directions while the young man, left alone, walked along toward the Egyptian.

As he walked along he heard two women talking and as the princess happened to be the subject of their conversation he sauntered more slowly so that he could hear what they were saying. The smaller one of the two said:

"I don't see where her wonderful preservation comes in, for she is nothing but a mummy anyhow. Anybody could be as stiff as she is if she had been soaked in coal tar a year or so. And they dry them so that they are nothing but a piece of tinder, and I am surprised that Mr. Huntington should think her remarkable. I am sure she cannot show a curl of real hair as soft and silky as it was when she was alive, like someone that I know of."

This caused the young man to notice the speaker more particularly, and he saw that while she was small, there was still something about her that made him think she had been a beauty in her lifetime, for the shape and the outlines of her head and skeleton were certainly different from those of most of the others. There was something of elegance in her movements and more grace than one could mentally connect with a skeleton. She held her head very much to one side and reminded him of the girls he had read about in the old romances, "bending over her tambour frame, with her eyes cast down modestly while her lovely eyes were suffused with tears of sensibility."

On one side of the head which was turned to the newspaper man there was a long curl of silky brown hair. This she twisted constantly with her bony fingers and smoothed with apparent affection, a sentiment which the young man understood when, by an unfortunate movement she half turned her head and he saw that there was not another spear of hair on her whole skull. Between a desire to laugh at the utter ridiculousness of her pretension, and pity for the little feminine vanity that made her cling to her one poor lone curl, the young man retired into the shadows made by the decorations, and that is how he happened to hear the conversation of several lady ghosts.

As soon as the banquet was finished, the Egyptian princess had been installed in her high chair, and she held audience with as many men as could crowd around her, and so the women were in a measure left to themselves. They gathered into groups and fell to discussing various subjects. Some told of what they had been doing the evening before, when they were abroad in their spiritual form only. One of them said sadly:

"I went to the place where my husband and I always loved to be. I thought perhaps he might be there, for he promised me as I lay dying that on every anniversary of my death he would go there. It was there that we had become engaged, and we were so happy there—"

"Did he come?" asked she of the lone curl.

"Yes; he did come, but he brought another woman with him, and the very things he used to say to me he said to her. He kissed her and told her that he had never loved anyone as he loved her, for such love comes but once in a lifetime. She is the fifth woman to whom I have heard him say the same things. I wish he would at least seek some other place for his foolishness, for you cannot imagine how foolish it seems to hear a man make love to another woman. He wouldn't be my choice of a man anyhow if I had my life to live over again. It will be a happy day when I get my passport and can leave all these worries behind."

Here was the question of passports again, and yet the newspaper man did not know what it meant. He began to blame himself for remissness in his duty, and to fear that he would find himself outside without having learned it. So he made up his mind that he would ask his host about it the first thing when he should find him again.

The second woman took up the conversation and said:

"Well, Mary, your lot is not so hard as mine. You had no little children to leave. When I died I went to my old home and hovered over my little children, knowing that they needed a mother's care, and there sat another woman beside the cradle, and it was she who answered when my baby cried. It was the first time the baby spoke and she called that woman mother."

At this moment the girl with the curl, as the reporter called her, began to complain again, but this time it was about the grave of Charlotte Temple.

"Really it wearies me to see what a ridiculous fuss all the lovelorn fools make about her grave. And, she got her passport long ago. Really I think that is paying a premium on weakness. One would think she was the only one to be disappointed in a man. Here come any number of silly things every day and nearly always bring something to put on her slab, which isn't much, anyhow. Not a word of epitaph, nothing but her name.

"The only thing good about it is that someone hollowed out a place so that birds can drink out of it. After a rain there may be some water there, but it soon dries up, and others bring flower pots and bouquets for poor Floyd to sweep away. I noticed tonight that there was a scrubby little fish geranium in a dried up pot standing there and a most forlorn little kitten was trying to find a few drops of water."

The young man instantly resolved that he would find that poor little kitten which, he felt sure, was the very one at which he had shied the stone. His mother would not object, so having set his conscience at rest, as so many of us do by promising to right a wrong—later on—he found himself again listening when one of the other women took up the conversation, and looking at the Egyptian, who still seemed to monopolize the gentlemen ghosts to a most scandalous extent and remarked:

"I think a woman as black as that mummy ought not to be allowed here among us. As to princesses of her time, they were no better than they should be, and if history is correct, they went about in such a state as to scandalize anybody. They certainly couldn't have been pretty with those black faces. And I, for one, don't think they should be set up for miracles either."

At this moment there passed a queer-looking woman ghost. Her back was bad and her legs were queer, like those of poor little Jenny Wren, and she had, in spite of her affliction, such a grand air of importance that she was remarkable among all the ghosts. As she passed the girl with the curl, she gave her head a toss as if she really intended an insult. As soon as she had passed out of hearing, the girl with the curl turned to the others and said:

"Did you see Mrs. Simon Mullinstalk? I imagine you will know her the next time you do, for she is so proud of that name that she tries to project her personality everywhere. Did you ever hear how she came by that magnificent name?"

"No," they all said in a chorus, "who is she, anyway?"

"Why she was an old maid, and her name was Susannah Skinks. She was the only daughter of old Solon Skinks. He had a snug little fortune, but was such a miser that they never had enough to eat. I have heard my mother say that it was working beyond her strength while she was small that she became as you see her. When her father died—her mother had died long before—he gave her all he had, on the promise that while she lived she would never marry anyone. She kept her promise, but when she lay upon her deathbed—she was then forty-eight years old—she for some reason felt that she did not wish to have her name and age go down to posterity on her tombstone as an old maid. She unbosomed her feelings to her pastor. He knew she had money and might remember the missionary work in which he was interested, and advised her, saying that she was practically dead now, and there could be no harm in making a deathbed marriage.

"They sent for the man whose name appealed to her. He was a hopeless paralytic, and had to be brought to her. They were left alone while she unfolded her plan to him. She wanted to be able to have 'Mrs.' on her tombstone, and if he consented to marry her now, she would will him everything she possessed. This just suited him, for the county had been supporting him for a long time, and he felt his position keenly. Here was a chance to suddenly become a man of importance, and from being a pauper, he could also provide for his old mother. As the minister was there and everything foreseen and provided for, the wedding was soon over and notice of it sent to the local paper. The old mother was sent for and Mr. Mullinstalk remained. Two days later she died. She had designed what she wished to have put on her tombstone. But when the sculptor went to carve the name, he somehow miscalculated the length of the name and could get only as far as Mrs. Simon Mullinst—, and carried the rest to a line below, but Simon seemed to think it was all right."

"Did she give anything to the missionaries?" asked an old lady with great interest.

"Not a penny, but she gave all her old clothes. That preacher was engaged to be married at the time and after the wedding they went off to some desolate place where the savages killed them. The cannibals were merciful enough to grant their last request, and that was that they should be boiled in the same kettle, and served up in the same dish, so that people could say of them that 'they were lovely in their lives and in death were not divided,' "

"It must have been an intolerable blessing, when they loved each other so. Poor critters! Well, they are having their reward, I hope."

Just then the tall ghost came along and spoke to the lady of the long, lone curl. He asked her if she would not like to take a turn, at the same time lifting her small hand in his, with exceeding care so as not to break any of the delicate bones. He said:

"My dear young lady, how glad I am of having the honor of seeing you once more. It makes me regret that things are as they are here, yet I find a balm for my hurt in the fact that there is no marrying, or giving in marriage, for thus I am assured that no one else can claim you. We can be friends until we get our passports, and possibly we shall be permitted to maintain the same friendly relations beyond."

At this delicate compliment, the maiden bowed her head and smiled, as indeed she had to, having no means of doing anything else. So, when the tall ghost offered his arm to take her around to see the decorations, she managed so skillfully that she took his right arm so that he should not see the bald side of her head. If he had seen it he could not have made any objections since his own head was as bare of hair as a stone. As they moved off the young man turned his attention again to the women and their conversation. He heard one say:

"I do not belong here, for I am buried in old St. Luke's, and if it hadn't been for the kindness of a friend I should have had nowhere to go tonight. I really wish we could stay dead and not have to come out until we are called for transfer. I never come out, but I am made to wish I hadn't. You know they have taken our peaceful resting place and made a public park of it, and that without being sure that we were all removed. Those of us without relatives left were removed by the Trinity Corporation, or at least that is what I was told. While they were moving the bodies, I remembered a verse that was written by someone who must have seen something like this. It runs:

"There's a grim one-horse hearse in a jolly round trot, To the churchyard a pauper is going, I wot; The road is rough and the hearse has no springs, And hark to the dirge which the mad driver sings: 'Rattle his bones over the stones, He's only a pauper whom nobody owns.'"

"Nobody seems to think that old bones can feel. What hurts me worst though is where it said on my monument, for I had a rather nice one for the period when I was buried, that 'she died at the age of 21 in the bloom of her youth and beauty, leaving her parents and her young husband desolate.' Yes;

my young husband remained desolate just one year and a day, and then he
married again. But as long as they lived my parents mourned for me. I tell you
what, my dears, a man's love for a woman lasts just as long as she is there
to make him comfortable, and no longer. I saw him not long ago, and he is
old and fat, bald and toothless, and he chews tobacco. Since then I have been
almost glad that I am dead. I wish I could get my passport, but I suppose I
have not learned all the lessons the Master has set for me."

"Do you believe that it is true that when we marry there is a truer union
than that between parents and children? You know that it says in the Bible,
'For this cause a man shall leave his father and his mother, and they twain
shall be one flesh.'"

Another woman who up to now had taken no part in the conversation
spoke in a resonant voice, and with a certain manner that betokened long
practice in public. She said impressively:

"Yes; we have all heard that, but I think the translators have got it mixed,
and it should not read shall, but will leave his father and mother, for we know
that he will do just as he likes and find a good reason for anything he wants
to do. And we do not need to be told how long it takes him to forget the wife
he declared he could not live without. And we can calculate to the hour when
he will remarry. The fact of the matter is that man is an utterly selfish being.
Women have been expecting too much of men. They should be taught that
women are not to be made the playthings of an idle hour. Oh, if we could only
advise our earthly sisters! Let us form a union—a strong union—and make
our displeasure felt at this outrageous infidelity. I will be president,"

There were murmurs of various kinds, none of them very distinct, and then
the lady continued;

"All of you who are in favor of the movement hold up your hands."

One large and still imposing woman ostentatiously folded her hands, and
several of the others followed her lead and kept their hands down. The
would-be president said:

"Madam, may I ask you if you have any personal objection to me?"

"None at all," was the reply.

"Then I beg that you will reconsider your antagonistic attitude and raise
your hand with the rest. Or, if you have any objection, please state it."

"I'll be tail to no one's kite, and don't you forget it."

This blunt reply caused three or four men who had unnoticed gathered
around, to break out into their queer crackling laughter, and this so incensed
the would-be president that she walked away in a most dignified manner. The
young man found that he had unconsciously formed the nucleus of a group
of men, and he felt glad of it, for there were several things that he felt he must

learn before the end of the evening. So as these men seemed to him to be kindly disposed, he said to one of them:

"I could not help hearing the complaints of those ladies, and it would give me the liveliest pleasure if I could learn something more of all this reunion. And, so far as I could judge by my own short experience and observation, women are quite as apt to remarry as men. I think they are a little harsh in their judgment."

"You are right, young man," said a fine, intellectual-looking ghost, "but there is something to be said on the other side. Women marry oftener than men after being widowed. If anything is said they claim a dozen reasons why it became a necessity. Being left alone and without support, they have to marry. If they have money they need someone to take care of it. Now I was married, and I assure you that had she died, I should have gone to my grave mourning for her. She promised me on my deathbed that she would not give any man even enough encouragement to allow him to ask her hand. I died content, and felt sure that some time we would be united in that better land. I willed her everything I had. By George! She came to my grave one day with a bunch of flowers and began to cry and tell me that she was lonely, and that she had seen a man who could cheer her up, and asked my consent to her marriage with him. Of course I could not speak to say no, and the artful minx took my silence as a tacit consent. Then she called me all sorts of a noble and generous man, and went off. The next day she came back with the silliest looking chump you ever saw, and she said to me lying there helpless down below: "Jim, you know that I promised you that I would never let any man propose to me, so now to show you that I have kept my word, I ask you, Reginald-Ethelbert, to be my husband." I was cured of all my infatuation for her as soon as I saw what kind of a man she thought so noble and so grand. They are both old now, and if I had wanted revenge, I could have had it, for they are about as well suited to each other as a cat and dog. It is better not to ask any promises, for a woman will find some way to get out of them, and it is still better not to regard wedlock as an indissoluble tie, for death does dissolve it, and we have been told that in Heaven there is no marrying or giving in marriage."

This was a new and comforting idea for the young man, and he began to feel that after all this life is short, and that it might not be long before the foreign count would be no more to the girl he loved so hopelessly than himself. Then he asked the ghost:

"Will you kindly tell me, sir, on what ground men and women meet in the sphere where you all ultimately go?"

"There are many things which we who are still in this intermediate existence do not know, but it is the general opinion that we shall meet upon one
platform of spiritual goodness, and be just friends.

"In life, if you think it over, there is nothing so sweet and worthy as true
friendship, and that obtains also in the world of spirits. There we shall all
be friends, true and faithful in the deepest meaning of the word. We shall
find the most exquisite pleasure in working for others, and as we are devoted
and self-sacrificing toward others, so will others be to us, and in that way the
peace and good will will so permeate all that the whole atmosphere will be
charged with the utmost delight."

"According to that belief there will be no love making, and those who
believed in their love for each other will not feel the same kind of sentiment
in the other world?"

"My young friend, as you now understand it, there is no love. There are on
earth natural selections, or affinities, and there are personal attractions, and
there are other and less noble instincts; vanity, interest, and a hundred other
mental conditions which we bunch together and call love. All of these, singly
or collectively, are disappointing from beginning to end. They are the cause of
more crime and misery than words can tell. Love, as we call it, is of this world,
and is not perfect. Eliminate the word love and put in its place pure and true
friendship, and we have heaven. Heaven, do you understand?"

"Some persons would prefer the world and the love that makes it turn
around," said the newspaper man rather flippantly, yet at the same moment
he felt a great throb of pain as the vision of the beautiful girl he so hopelessly
loved flashed through his mind. The ghost, with a gentle bend of his head,
said:

"You are thinking of Miss ____, and being also of the earth my words fall
upon impatient ears, but there will come a day when all earthly desire shall
have faded from your mind and heart, you will find that a pure and sweet
friendship is far more satisfying than any present love could be. So keep your
heart pure and be true to yourself, and your time of probation will be short.
She will be there before you, and when your heart is laid bare before her—"

"But I said nothing about any young lady," said the young man, half frightened as he suddenly remembered that fact.

"I know you did not," replied the ghost, "We do not require that anyone
should speak, though we do talk to each other, but that is more from force of
habit than necessity. And, especially where the theme is one of deep import,
one uplifting in its subject, we simply sense what another would say."

"Sir," said the reporter, "I should be glad of any information that you can
conscientiously give me about life after death and the future existence."

"It is a natural sentiment, but I fear there is little left for you to know. You have been permitted to penetrate to the abode of the dead and to behold all there is to see. You find that men and women can come out of their coffins, walk about and converse, eat and drink, and later you may see them at their penance. You have probably noticed that they are all possessed of a certain resemblance to what they were in life—that is, they have their bony structure still, and something of their personality, and much of their disposition. So long as the bones do not decay they must stay under the conditions as you see them. The decay of the bones seems to be regulated by the character of the owner of them, and the use he made of them in his lifetime. So long as there is any of the material part of the body left the spirit is chained to it, though it may leave it for a time when the spiritual longing is stronger than the material in the bones. When we get our passports the whole dissolves, and we here long for that consummation. Ah, much more than I can tell you."

CHAPTER VI
THE GHOSTS TELL STORIES, AND COMPARE NOTES

AT THIS MOMENT ANOTHER ghost came up and joined in the conversation and said impressively: "Young gentleman, you are having the most remarkable experience of your life. You want to see all you can, for probably never before did man come down and see the dead as they really are—before they get their passports. Certainly some live persons do come down occasionally, but they do not count, for they are only those who are buried alive, and they do not get out, as they do not as a rule live long. All these ghosts are dead of body, but are not sufficiently purified in soul to go free from the hindrance of bones. So they all, men and women alike, are burdened with many of their old characteristics, and in many ways they act much as they did during life. Indeed, it has seemed to me that it may be quite possible that the repetition of their least pleasant characteristics here is a sort of punishment, and—well, all this will doubtless strike you as different from what you had imagined. It shall be my pleasant task to tell you anything you may wish to know so far as it lies in my power."

"I should like to know very much whether you ever want to see your families, and how you manage to see them, and how it is that you seem to know everything that goes on above ground."

"We lie here in the dark alone, for except for this one night in the year our bones are imprisoned in our coffins, or wherever we lie, if, as many of us have no coffins to lie in. That silence and isolation naturally creates a necessity for thought, concentrated and intense. This thought is most often connected with those whom we have left, and with whom we have been the most closely associated in life, and so the thought becomes desire. Thoughts are things, and they crystallize into a vehicle for our transportation to wherever we wish to go. We then become in a measure disassociated from the material part of ourselves, and the freed spirit can go where it will, and as it retains its ego, it is as a general rule anything but pleasant to go and hover around places and persons we have left. Sometimes it has occurred to me that some of our punishment was thus intended.

"In my life I was one of that kind of men that thought the world could not go on without me, and I was sure that my death would leave a void that never could be filled. And, above all, I thought that all my well-laid plans for the benefit of my family would be allowed to relapse into confusion. All I ever did for my family was to advise them, and the only real benefit I ever conferred upon them was by dying, so that they could collect the insurance I had placed on my life. Well, I have since been obliged to float around in space, unnoticed and unheard, and probably unremembered, while things were being done which would have had no approbation from me, and they came out right after all. I am obliged to admit that my family and the world at large have gained by my death. Yet I was a very religious man and was class leader in church, and always had prayers every morning before breakfast. I am ashamed to tell you the epitaph they put on my stone, but I must admit in the light of what I know now I deserved much worse."

"I should like very much to know what it was," said the reporter eagerly.

"Very well; I will repeat it, leaving out the 'here lies,' etc.: 'He gave Each day to Almighty God, advice of considerable worth; But his wife Took in sewing to keep him going, While he superintended the earth.'"

"But it is much when you get to such a point that you see what were your shortcomings in the upper world." "How much of it is out?" said another ghost who was standing by interested in this recital.

"Oh, you know that is truth and so is easy."

"I suppose we all have shortcomings against our record when it comes to count all the things we did and didn't do to our wives. We seemed to think that when we had married a woman there was nothing further to do to make her happy, and the better and more willing she was the more we imposed upon her. I was rather bossy myself, and I thought as you did that this world could not get along without me, and I guess I must have carried my bossiness a little too far. One morning Marinthy was tired of it and fixed a plan that made me a little ashamed, for the time. She slipped out of bed before daylight and set all the clocks ahead four hours and then rang the dinner bell and when the family had all gathered she told them that she did not know what was going to happen now, for their father had forgotten to tell the Lord that it was time for the sun to rise."

"You are not the only one to have a rise taken out of you, for I had a little of that sort of experience myself," said another ghost with a very long under jaw. "I, too, liked to lay down the law for all my family to obey. My wife was generally a meek little soul, and never questioned my right to order even the most trifling things. But, at last she revolted and one day during protracted meetings when two clergymen and the vestryman of our church were at my house to dinner and we were all in the parlor waiting for it to be ready, she opened the door half way and crept timidly into the parlor, with a meek and browbeaten air, and asked permission of me to breathe through her mouth as her nose was stopped up."

Everybody within hearing laughed at this, but the ghost who had told it, and he glared at the first speaker, but they happened to think of something else and calmed down. One of them turned to the reporter, saying: "Is there anything that you would like to know more than we have told you?"

"Yes; you said that you could float around and see all that is going on. I should like to know if any one of your friends feels or in any way recognizes your presence?"

"They do not. We are intangible and invisible, and there is nothing to show them that we are there, and the most ridiculous side of it is that every one would be scared nearly to death if he or she knew that there was a spirit in the room. Then is the time that they need have the least fear, for there is nothing of us that could do the least possible harm."

"Are there no persons whose natures are so attuned to the spiritual life that they can see you or feel your presence, and keep silent?"

"If there is one I do not know him or her, and frankly, I do not think that any one ever saw a spirit. There is nothing to see. As to the return of disembodied spirits to their old habitations, that is certainly true, but no one knows it or can know it, and so it does no harm and no special good."

Here the first speaker took up the question and said: "I believe that we can influence some dreams by entering into the mind of one who sleeps and is therefore in a measure free from all earthly thrall save life itself. I know that three times I have been able to enter into the mind of my daughter in her sleep, and I have impressed her so that she has shown clearly that she recognizes my direction. But her case is a peculiar one, as she is one whose mind is absorbed to a degree by her work so that every waking thought is occupied with it and she elects to be alone as much as she can. Being thus removed from most outside influences and having no distractions aside from her own thoughts, and having what one might define as an indwelling nature, as well as a highly sensitive organization, she has become almost like a sensitized photographic plate, only it is in her brain that she receives these unconscious impressions in her sleep. When she awakens she believes she has dreamed, but the impression is so strong that she obeys the line of conduct laid out for her in this way. She feels somehow that it is from me that the direction comes, and acts on it. But, from all that I have heard this is an exceptional case."

"I think so, too," said the other ghost, "and now you know as much about that as we do. We are but the bones and a few ligaments, and we are waiting until such time as may suit the Master to give us release, and move us to whatever sphere of existence He may choose."

At this moment a ghost stepped up and said in a brisk way, as though he belonged to a newer and more active age: "Gentlemen," here he bowed to the newspaper man, and then right and left, "what these gentlemen have said is quite true, as my own experience will show, and if this gentleman wishes I will tell my own story." The young man bowed and said that he certainly should like to hear it, so the ghost said:

"That we can come out of our mouldering bodies and hover unseen about our own homes is so. About six months after I was dead I was seized with the most intense longing to go to my house. I have been dead but a comparatively short time. I had been married but about two years and naturally hated to leave my young wife. But—well—we are not always free agents in these cases and must die when our time comes. I was run over by a cable car," he added as he saw that all nearby seemed to be interested, and particularly the young man. "I was killed soon after the Spanish war broke out. I did not want to go as a volunteer and risk being shot and killed. I had a good business all my own and a nice little home all paid for, and I had every reason to wish to live. My wife thought I ought to leave all that and strike for glory. I tried to make her see that glory does not go to the unit, but to the officers in command, but it was no use, she kept it up. I could not go anywhere without hearing bands of music and seeing soldiers, and at last it annoyed me so that I would take any chance to avoid it. And, that is just how I came to be killed. I started to cross a street when one car was coming up and another going down, I never did know just how it happened, but the wheels went over my neck. You may notice how loose it is."

"What did you do? How did you feel? When did you know that you were dead? Or did you know nothing until they got you out?" began the reporter breathlessly, for somehow this accident appealed to him in an unusually strong way.

"I knew as soon as I was out of my body. I watched them lift the car with jacks to get me out. I felt so mad that anger swallowed up every other sensation to think I had let myself be killed in this senseless way. But it was no use. I followed along and was in the house ahead of my body, and found Mary sitting there surrounded with half a dozen scarehead newspapers around her reading about the war. They brought my body in, and you never saw such heartrending grief. I felt sorry for her, but I could do nothing. She sobbed and moaned and screamed with hysterics, and it took four persons to hold her. Of course it was a shock, I admit that, but it need not have made her such an idiot."

"I think her grief quite natural," said the reporter.

"Of course, of course. But wait till I tell you the rest. They sent for an undertaker, one of the swell ones. Common funerals are out of date now, or you would have thought so had you heard him talk. Honey from Hymettus was not sweeter than his sympathy, and oil from the olive groves of Italy was not so smooth as his tongue. He was so gentle and suggestive in his consolatory words that before the poor girl understood she had given him carte blanche to have a funeral such as should show the proper amount of respect for the dead and her uncontrollable grief. Oh, yes; everything must be such as would pour balm into that broken heart. She had never wanted anything during my life, and she knew absolutely nothing about business, so that glib fellow just turned her around his finger. The funeral must be in church. That meant the music and preacher to pay besides all the other things. There must be palms all down the aisle, and floral pieces. I must be embalmed. Well—I hope he may be obliged to float helplessly around and see some other fellow embalm him. And I hope it may be a business rival! My coffin was the finest, copper-lined, with silver handles and plate-glass top. And she agreed to it all without asking the price. She did not know enough.

"Well, I suppose I ought to feel flattered about it, but I don't. No, sir! And then the grave. The highest priced lot was chosen by that wily undertaker, and the grave dug. An awning was stretched over it, and all the earth that came out was sifted so that it should fall lightly without that sickening thud that we hear when the clods strike the coffin. Folding chairs were there for the mourners, and iced vichy for those who were thirsty. Carriages were provided for every Tom, Dick and Harry that wanted to have a free ride. My wife was the only mourner, for we neither had any relatives. But, my employees were there, and every comfort was provided for them. I am telling you this to show how women are imposed upon. Why the crape upon the door was a yard wide and twice as long. The undertaker made his strong point always saying that nothing less would be showing the proper respect. And my own dress suit that I hadn't worn but three times was not good enough, and so he went and put another on and charged her a hundred dollars extra.

"While he was doing this my wife had let her friends go to the swellest store in the city and order her mourning. They did not have to pay for it themselves, and it felt important to be ordering the best. Nothing short of the finest and richest Eudora cloth was good enough for the dress, and this had to be almost covered with the heaviest Courtauld crape, like those worn for court mourning abroad, and among the smart set here. Her bonnet had a little roll of white in front to show that she was a widow, and there was veil of the crape over the bonnet that reached the feet back and front, and was reefed up in a deep fold or hem or whatever they call it. Then there were gloves and black bordered handkerchiefs, and dull black jewelry, and to top off with a long sealskin coat. They told her that was the fashionable fur, for mourning, and it was better to get a good one while she was about it, as it would always be useful. They paid eight hundred dollars for that!

"What is the use talking any more about it. She paid her respects to the dead in the same kind of clothes the millionaires wear, but it took the house and lot to pay for them, and crippled the business besides. That undertaker soaked her for three thousand dollars, and took a mortgage on the house and furniture to pay, and the business went to the dogs in less than six months. I used to go up and hover around and try to infuse a little sense into her head, but it was no use. I don't go there any more."

This last was said with such evident dejection that the reporter asked sympathetically why he had ceased his visits.

"Well, it is this way. One evening about six months after my death, as I was saying, I went there and found her sitting at the piano and playing softly and talking between bars to a young woman whom I had never liked. She was really the principal one to lead Mary on in her fatal extravagance.

"From her conversation I found that the mortgage was to be foreclosed the next week. The business was at its last gasp, and I thought she seemed more cheerful than circumstances warranted. Well, to make a long story short she was telling her friend that she was engaged to marry a captain in the army and that as soon as her year and day was finished they would be married and go to Porto Rico where he was to be stationed. Well, sir, I was so mad that I did not know what to do. All I could do was to stand there behind the piano and listen to their gabble. I never went back again. I don't care if she has to take in washing to support him. Now, wouldn't that make your hair curl?"

"I certainly think it would," replied the newspaper man earnestly. Just then a small sized ghost stepped forward timidly and in a very polite manner bowing and signifying that he did not wish to intrude, yet had something to say. Several were gathered there and each evidently intended to tell the story of his own taking off.

"Sir," said the little man as soon as he saw that the reporter noticed him, "perhaps you might feel interested in the singular way in which I came to die. I may almost say that I did another man's dying for him."

"It would be very interesting, I am sure," replied the young man with a bow. This ghost had a heavy manzanita cane with abundant evidence of the hard knotty roots at the knob, and they were so very sharp that the simple appearance of it was quite enough to provoke interest in the story, so the little ghost heaved a deep sigh and began:

"I will make my story as short as possible, as time presses. I was a young man in the best of health, when some forty-five years ago I started to California to make my fortune. I intended to start a jewelry store in one of the mining towns, in fact Murphy's Camp, a place well known then as it is now. Some of the story I did not know myself at the time of my death, though I learned it since and will incorporate it in this.

"The people of that part of the country liked to play practical jokes on strangers—I was a stranger—and they took me in. The stage driver and all the passengers set out to frighten me with the most blood-curdling tales of the way travelers were robbed and murdered for their money or belongings. As I had all my stock with me I felt very nervous. I did not know that all this was what they called 'Joshing green horns.' So by the time we reached Murphy's I was scared all the way through.

"We reached there just at sundown, and as soon as supper was over I went to my room and to bed. I was very tired. This room was partitioned off with redwood boards and was not even papered. There was just room for a narrow bed, a small stand and one chair. I put all my things under the bed, but I lay awake a long time, on account of strange mutterings and moans and cries in one of the rooms. But at last I fell asleep.

"I must now tell you what I learned afterward regarding the affair. I was an Englishman, small in size, and my hair was red and very curly. There was in this town another English jeweler, small and with curling red hair. He had had typhoid fever for several days and it was his delirious moans I heard.

"All the miners of this place gathered every evening at the barroom of this hotel, at the time of which I speak, to pass the time and play cards. Sometimes they remained until morning. The driver of the coach was an enormous man, strong as an ox, and as good-natured. He was a regular fanatic about the game they call poker, and they say he would play forty-eight hours on a stretch. They tell a story about how he and another poker fiend kept on playing once till their cards began to smoke before they knew the place was on fire.

"Seeing that this driver was settled for the night the hotel keeper asked him if he would do something for him. 'Certainly, what is it?' The other replied that the little English jeweler was very sick, and that he was worn out taking care of him. So he asked the driver to give the sick man his medicine at exactly three o'clock. The driver was always willing to do anyone a good turn, and asked about the dose, and how to prepare it, saying at the same time that the little Englishman must have been taken very suddenly. The landlord replied that he had indeed and was scarcely expected to pull through, and that all depended on his getting his medicine regularly. 'And, he will tell you that he isn't sick, and don't want any medicine, and all that, but you must make him take it.'

"'All right,' replied the driver, 'I'll see that he takes it. You go to bed.' They played and smoked until three o'clock, and then the big driver mixed up the draught in a big spoon, and taking a candle he came up the stairs. He forgot about the other Englishman, and asked the porter where the little Englishman was that had come up that day. The sleepy porter told him where my room was. Now I can tell the rest from my own knowledge. I was suddenly aroused from my sleep to see an enormous form standing beside my bed, outlined by the flickering candle on the stand, and naturally my first thought was that I was about to be robbed and murdered, perhaps murdered first. I called out to know who it was and the big figure said:

"'You keep still now, and don't get excited. No one is going to hurt you, so just take this now, and then lie down and go to sleep. It won't hurt you.'

"I was sure now that I was going to be drugged into insensibility and I told him that I would take nothing. He said:

"'Now don't you fash yourself, but take this medicine, It will do you good and is not bad to take, all stirred up with molasses.'

"'But I won't touch it,' I cried; 'you want to drug me and rob me. Get out of here.' As I said that I pushed him away with all my strength, but he just put his great hand around my neck and jerked me up in bed, saying:

"'Ah, I knew you would say that. Now come on and no more nonsense.' With that he jammed the spoon down my throat and choked me with the other hand so that I had to swallow or strangle. So I took his dose, and he let me go, and laid me down in bed again like a baby, but I think I fainted, for I knew nothing more until the daylight was streaming in the window. I found all my things untouched, but I felt awfully ill, and could scarcely get up. But I determined to leave, if they would let me, as soon as I could get away. When I did get down stairs everybody had heard of the affair and they began to make fun of me. I took passage back to Stockton, but I felt very queer. I took cold and died in about six weeks, and the other Englishman got well. The shock and the awful dose combined with the cold I took finished me up. What made me the maddest of all was that the doctor I had in Stockton was some kind of a foreigner, and he could not write English. So, my death was written down as having been caused by 'Gallumpin consumpsin'."

The whole assemblage of ghosts who were listening to this tale of woe agreed that death sometimes has sharper stings than we know. The ghosts with whom the newspaper man had been talking before this interruption now gathered around him again and he thought that probably now was his chance to learn something of the question so often mentioned of "getting the passports." That there was to be a move onward toward some desired goal he felt sure and at the risk of seeming importunate he asked of the nearest one:

"Sir, is it permitted you to give me any information regarding the next move onward, or upward, or whatever you call it, or what you mean when you speak of your passports? I need not tell you how much I desire to understand this."

"My dear sir, you know as much about it as we do. We all dread it while we still desire it sincerely. We dread it because we do not know what it will be, but on the other hand we wish the change, hoping that it will be a step toward better things. There are some reasons of which we prefer not to speak, why we would welcome a change. Anyone who pretends to know more than this is a liar. You see we use strong words down here, for truth is a fundamental principle of life after death, and we are trying to practice it."

"And you might add," said one of the ghosts who had been talking when the man told of his sudden taking off and his grievance against the undertaker. "You might add that no spirit would or could harm anyone, for in the first place he has not the power, and secondly he thinks more of trying to undo the evil he did in lifetime than to do more,"

"Just one thing more I should like to ask, and that is if there is ever any kind of religious service or observance down here?"

The newspaper man was growing bolder as he became better acquainted with the ghosts, and had the welcome assurance that they would not harm him.

"There is no religion as you have been taught to consider it in any of the underground places," replied the ghost. "It will surprise some of the preachers when they come down to learn even the little we know. They preach one thing, but when they get here they will find that truth in all things, love to your neighbor, and charity to all is all that is required of us, and I believe all that is essential to give us a chance to work out our own salvation."

"And for punishment? Is there a hell as we have been taught? And, what must we do to be saved? Must we join some church, and if so what one?"

"All churches lead to one goal. As it is, the One who created us has given us all a chance to work out our own salvation after we are dead. We can go on being ghosts, which means unredeemed souls for a few million years and redeem ourselves. But it is hard—very hard—to overcome our sins and weaknesses. As near as I can make it out there is a constant advance toward perfection in everything. It began uncounted millions of years ago, and will continue to all eternity. Evolution, the survival of the fittest, and all those things have truth for foundation, though the men who have been the ones to advance those theories have but the faintest glimmering of the truth. But I think from all I have seen and heard that Hell is that period of our existence while we are still chained to existence, obliged to know all that goes on without power to hinder or help. I used to preach other theology when I was a bishop, but I see things now with my spiritual instead of earthly eyes. I think I may say that this short life as men and women, is fraught with more meaning than any of our previous existences in different forms—for in this life we have been pretty nearly free agents—and a pretty mess we have made of it all. We shall have a chance to progress to higher—meaning better—conditions when we shall be sufficiently purified, or at least I hope so."

"And, is there no special punishment, like frying in a cauldron of boiling pitch and things like that?" asked the young man somewhat anxiously, thinking at the same time of Dante's Inferno, which he had just been reading.

"No, but there are such things as moral suffering, and one thing came to my knowledge today. This is what one might call poetic justice, and it would be comic if it were not so tragic. It is this; all the women who have deliberately and with intention shirked the cares of maternity while alive, are obliged to take care of the children of the poor overworked women whose quivers were full of them on earth. There is a kind of heavenly kindergarten, but the labors of these nurses and teachers are quite as hard as were those of the poor mothers, and the unaccustomed and often unpleasant labor is enough to make any poor rich woman shed tears of rage and worry—that is, if it were a possible thing for a ghost to cry—for the source of their tears is dried up forever. I heard one woman say that she would give one million years of heaven if she could only have one good cry."

"So then there is none of that weeping and wailing and gnashing of teeth that we read about and have dinned into our ears ever since we could hear, and long before we could understood?"

"No; but don't think that you can do wrong with impunity. Ex fatoris, is the law, and it is always enforced in one way or another. But, we are here tonight to enjoy ourselves as well as the nature of the occasion will permit. Each has full permission to follow his or her own inclinations, and—well—some of them seem to forget that they are adding to their own term of detention. We have been talking on subjects usually avoided by people on pleasure bent, and I should not have said so much only that I hope it may do some good directly or indirectly. The music will soon begin to play for those who wish to dance, and after that we shall have a short convention, where some important questions will be discussed with a view to interest the living public in our needs and complaints."

"Before you leave me," said the young man hurriedly, "I beg you to tell me where the children are. I have not seen one, and I know that there are many buried right here and others in St. Paul's, and in all other cemeteries in the city."

"Children are never put under the same conditions as ours, and they are taken at once to an intermediate place and classed off, according to their ages, and they are happy in their own way. They are not allowed to remember anything about their previous existence. They are never enlightened as to the world and its miseries, and no one knows that it had parents or pain. They are all equal, and all are ignorant of sin or its punishment. They always remain little children. In short, all and every one who has not yet reached a state of sinlessness must pass through a period of purification, which I may say is purely mental, and only the Master knows how long or short it will be. Some that we thought would have to stay millions of years underground have all gone on long ago. Others who bore the very odor of sanctity are here yet. The Master has given every one a chance to save himself, each after his kind. I could never understand, even when I was officiating as bishop, how it was that such a comparatively small number of persons were to be saved from perdition, and I could not feel that a loving Father and our Creator could have left countless billions to die unredeemed, and then send them to that terrible hell for not knowing something which He had made it impossible for them to know. I used to wonder then, I do not now."

"Will you tell me? I suppose you mean the Heathen."

"Yes; I mean the Heathen, at home and in far lands. Ah, my young friend, we all try to find a short cut to heaven. I can only say love your neighbor, tell the truth, think only pure thoughts, and trust the rest to the Master. He created us all, the Jew and the Gentile, the Heathen and these calling themselves Christians. They are all alike to Him.

"Do you not see that a merciful Father, loving his own creation could not condemn them to everlasting tortures for not believing something that he himself had made it impossible for them to know? You must follow the same road, and work for your passport to the next place or phase of existence, which we all hope will be better, but of which we are as ignorant as you."

At this moment there was a faint and tremulous sound, indescribably sweet, and no one could have told from whence it came, but it grew in volume, and in a few minutes it had swelled louder and began to throb with the strange thrill that makes dance music so enlivening. As soon as the music was well under way it seemed to be the signal for every one to begin to talk. The noise was deafening, and the young man wondered how just ghosts could make so much confusion. He noticed three men who had evidently found the buffet, and they had evidently made the most of their find, for they would have been considered drunk in any other place. They were inclined to be noisy and quarrelsome, and the young visitor feared they would pick him out for punishment, but they seemed to ignore his presence. The bishop who had been talking to him said:

"You see that we are still full of the leaven of unrighteousness. Ah; there goes the most unsociable ghost I ever saw. He will never get away from here at that rate. He thinks he is just the biggest frog in the pond. Nobody likes him. That tall man over near him is next to him the most disagreeable ghost here. He is so swelled up with his own importance that he is looking with a candle for insults to his dignity. But, deary me! Here am I, a bishop too, gossiping like an old woman. I could be in better business, but some folks think they are the whole bunch. I heard that expression once—in fact, recently—and it struck me as being so forcible that—ah, me; I am forced to admit that a bishop is no more when he gets before the Master than any other man. And if he has not been better than the most of them he gets the same treatment. I used to think I was some value to the world, but bishops are nothing more or less than men down here. It has taken over two hundred years to make me admit that much. I used to stand among other men and take their reverential words as my just due, and when we were at the banqueting board I took the best of everything as my right indisputable and just. Now I take what I can get and must be content, for, as I said, all that has passed away. You see, we have outgrown preachers down here, and I often wonder why we ever had them. To change the subject, what are your impressions of what you see here tonight?

"It would be impossible to define them, for I see so much that put all my preconceived notions to flight that it will take long before I can really understand them myself. I am sure that I shall profit by your discourse," answered the reporter, earnestly, for the bishop's conversation did give him food for reflection.

Very opportunely one of the ghosts who had visited the buffet too often got into a wrangle, and no one knew how it happened but the young stranger, and he kept a discreet silence, for it was not his quarrel anyhow, but he had heard one ghost say to another:

"I notice that your name is obliterated—"

He got no further, for the other doubled up his fists and cried indignantly:

"You're a liar! My name is Jones, and don't you forget it."

The first speaker was ready for a fight, but the other ghosts surrounded them and tried to persuade Jones that the offending word was intended for a compliment, and begged him to overlook it, so finally they shook hands and sat down in a corner and promptly went to sleep.

The music now struck up a grand march and the ghosts formed in couples and marched to the music, and in perfect unison. The procession appeared interminable. The ghosts floated rather than walked. It seemed as if millions passed along.

The people in the procession were about as well assorted as one finds them in all marches, some being tall with short partners, and vice versa. Some walked smoothly and with a certain degree of dignity while others tried to take fancy steps reminding him of a cake walk. Four persons there were who did not join in the march, a young lady ghost, a tall man, the Egyptian princess and the newspaper man.

The young lady referred to had a timid and bashful air, and the man a gloomy bend of the head and a morose crossing of the arms over his bony chest, while the Egyptian was so enveloped in her wrappings that she would have found locomotion difficult. Besides she was seated to watch the proceedings. She rather liked being set up there, as something more and better than the rest, and she was not blind to the fact that all the other women were as jealous of her as they could be.

The newspaper man resumed his interrupted journey toward her, keeping carefully out of the way of the dancers, until he approached the princess, and with a profound bow began a conversation with her. He was not quite sure of the proper way to address her, as she was a princess, of no one knew what dynasty. And, a ghost besides. So, he naturally felt a little timid, but as she seemed to smile affably he began, at the same time taking out his note book and pencil from force of habit. Then he remembered where he was and hastily hid them again, and thanked his stars that no one had seen them, and recklessly said:

"Oh, most noble and highly exalted princess," here he stuck fast and did not know how to continue, but she deigned to smile on him. Indeed she had to smile for the embalmer who had made a mummy of her had fixed that charming smile on her lips with coal tar or whatever it was that they used for the purpose. But, whatever it was it served its purpose, and the princess smiled.

"Approach, young man" she said gently. He drew near and took hold of the bony but small and well shaped hand and was about to give it a hearty shake, but he remembered in time that it was the custom to kiss the hands of sovereigns, and he was not sure enough of her rank to take any chances, so he thought it better to make the mistake on the right side. So he knelt and kissed the hand held out to him, while his hair stood on end at that cold and stony contact. He wondered if in some occult way he had not bound himself to her through eternity. She broke the charm by saying in a voice as sweet as any one could wish to hear:

"Sir, be good enough to tell me in what way I can serve you, for I see question in your eyes and desire in your heart?"

This did not reassure him, for he did not half like the idea that all his thoughts were so evident, but he tried to do the best he could under the circumstance by saying lamely:

"Most noble of princesses, I will not try to disguise from your highness that I should be most grateful if you would tell me something about your illustrious self and how you came to this country and anything you may have seen in your long pilgrimage. Your highness must have seen many things that the world would like to know. The master of ceremonies said that you are more than five thousand years old, yet I find you young and beautiful—" Here the reporter stopped and strangled, for he happened to remember that she could read his thoughts, and he had said in his mind, 'Now we shall see how long a woman remains susceptible to flattery," and the cold sweat broke out on his forehead, but she only smiled more graciously than before, and said:

"I now perceive that you are not one of those vulgar curiosity seekers like those who tore me from my tomb, where I had hoped to sleep until my summons came. There is very little to tell. I have seen but about four thousand and nine hundred and fifty years, so I am not so old by considerable as that gentleman said, and doubtless in good faith. But, I have seen nations, races and armies melt away so that no trace of their existence remains, no stone of their habitations is seen above ground, and I have seen lands change their boundaries and the new rise up out of the old. Kings and queens have become dust and buried so deep in it that no one can tell where they were. Yes; I have seen so much that it would require a lifetime to tell you the half."

"Ah, did your highness ever see Cleopatra? She has always been a prominent figure in Egyptian history—and—she has been much discussed. I should like to know something of her from a contemporary."

"Oh," she replied stiffly, "I scarcely know to which Cleopatra you refer. There were several of them, but I suppose you refer to she who reigned last and was the cause of the overthrow of the nation, and who killed herself with an asp."

"Yes, your highness, that is the one," replied the young man eagerly.

"Well, in the first place, that queen is entirely too modern, and she reigned something like three or four hundred years before the Christian era, while I came from the family of one of the first of the real Egyptian sovereigns. She was not even Egyptian, being only of Greek origin. We did not recognize her when she died and she was not even mummified, for the Romans would not have allowed it, and so no one ever knew what ever really became of her body. It did not interest us, as she was an upstart who had brought all sorts of evils upon my country. She is doubtless dust and ashes two thousand years ago. She was greatly overrated, and was nowhere near so beautiful as she has been considered. I belonged to the first dynasty, though there had been many kings and queens before me. My tomb was like those of the first royal ladies of my line. I had never been married—nor had I reigned, so according to usage, my tomb and sarcophagus were plain, save for the paintings on them to tell who I was. One day some vandals came and rifled my tomb and took my mummy case, and brought it to this country and put me in the museum in a glass case, and you have no idea how angry it makes me to have to squeeze out. May the jackals eat their bones, and leave no two of them together, so they will never find them in this world or the other and may wild beasts tear their children, and leave the mothers desolate, and raze their dwellings, and may their babes starve to death, and may they all die crying for water—"

How much longer this would have continued the newspaper man did not know, but he began to feel most uncomfortable, for one of these very collectors of mummies was his own father, and if he had not brought his particular one he had brought two others. He began to want to go home, but he tried to look sympathetic, and as if he had never heard of such terrible things as stealing mummies before. She continued:

"Yes; I am lady Shep, and when I was mummified these lines were put upon my case. Not everybody knows about them, but I will tell you. First, there was a line of text, and this is what it says:

"Royal offering of Osiris Unifer (the good being), great lord god of Abydos, may he give every good thing, libations to the Ka (Double) of the Osiris, the lady of the house, the honorable Shep (justified).' This means that I lay a day and a night in the underground temple in the arms of Memnon, and all the good deeds I had done were weighed, and when they were found to be more than the evil ones I was justified. On the other side was this inscription: "The worthy mistress and daughter of Ru-ru, Justified; her mother was the lady of the house, Tarerust, Justified, and worthy.' On the left is another with the goddess Maat, and there are other gods and goddesses, all saying that Shep, the lady of the house, is justified and worthy of a place among the illustrious dead. We did not have to go under the same peculiar conditions as do you who have a different way of burial and belief. Perhaps because our bodies are made imperishable we come under another division. I cannot tell, but this I know, I slept peacefully when I should and did no harm when I came out at the command, and then the explorers as they call them, came and took me from my country so far away that I shall never see it more."

"Is there no way by which you could go back?" asked the young man, touched by her sorrow.

"No: for the scientific men would never let me go. Because my mummy case is the best one they have, and I am told that men of science have no honor and no feeling where it concerns the despoiling of tombs, whether they be of our people, or the red Indians who have built mounds or the Mexicans, or the old Peruvians. And, besides, we ghosts cannot cross the ocean in spirit form unless our bones go too."

"May I ask why?" questioned the young man, really distressed by what he heard, and now understood as he could not have done a day, even a few hours before.

"Because the spirit is an essence, and the cold of the water chills it, and renders it powerless to float, and so I can never behold the dear country of my birth again."

"What if I stole your mummy from the museum and took it back to Egypt?" said the young man, carried away by sympathy.

"We have often talked of just such a contingency nights up there, and we all agreed that if ever we did find any one who was willing to try, he might be beheaded after unheard-of tortures by the authorities of the museum, but if one could succeed we would make him the richest man in the world. We know many secrets. What if I told you that I know where the kings of the first and second dynasties got their gold and precious stones? I know where kings of the second dynasty got emeralds in such profusion that we scarcely cared for them. I was dead then, but I suppose that a woman never quite loses her interest in gems. I could take you to a place where you could get all the finest emeralds that you could carry."

This particularly appealed to him as the emerald was his birth stone, according to the astrologers, and besides he liked them better than any other. He remembered also that emeralds were the fashionable stones for the time, and that a fine emerald was worth more than a diamond of the same size. Therefore he was impressed.

He asked her when he could see her again and she answered that it must be just one whole year before she could come out of her sarcophagus in visible form, and when he wanted to try to communicate with her spirit she told him that such a thing was impossible, and had never been done by any spirit that ever floated. But he could come to the museum a year from then and manage somehow to stay in the building over night, and they could then discuss the situation, and see if some way could not be found by which she could be returned to her country. The young man thought if he could manage to get enough of this wealth of jewels to handle he could find some way to buy up the attendants. But he felt delicate about speaking of such a plan, for fear she would not understand that he didn't dare anything so dangerous without having money enough to silence all scruples of the night watchmen. He also thought to himself that probably no other man living had ever made two appointments like the two he had made this night; one to bring the good natured ghost a bottle of rum and a package of tobacco, and another with a mummy in a museum to make arrangements to steal her and carry her back to Egypt. It was enough to make one's hair stand on end. He thought he might be able to fix it with the ghost so that he could deposit the things in some safe place, because he felt that the affair with the princess was the more important. He was about to discuss the plan more fully when the grand march ended and the floor manager shouted:

"There will now be given a selection of the newest songs, such as are sung in the theaters above ground. You are requested to listen quietly, or if you must talk let it be in whispers, for it is very disconcerting for a singer to be interrupted by conversation during the time he is trying to amuse you."

The invisible band began to play and a man stepped out in the middle of the floor, while all the others formed a circle around him. They were so many that no one could have counted them, and all kept an expectant attitude, so that the words just uttered seemed quite unnecessary. As the music continued he was astonished to find that it was a rag-time dance and "coon song" combined just as he had seen only a few days ago in one of the theaters. As the man sang this the whole assembly took it quite seriously and applauded him with the rhythmic regularity of a theatrical claque, and then the same ghost bowed with a certain grace and to a persistent encore he stepped forward and began a cake walk, accompanied by a song about kissing your baby. The whole thing was so ludicrous that he nearly had a fit in trying not to laugh. He dared not give way to mirth, for they all seemed to take the matter so seriously that he was not sure as to what might happen to him. The princess was quite amused by this song and dance, and after the applause was over he asked her if she would like to dance, and she replied that none but slaves danced in her country, and they did so simply to amuse their owners. He was still under the stimulus of suppressed laughter and regarded the invitation as a good joke, but he would have changed his mind if she had not said sweetly:

"Of course you could not know it, but princesses could not so demean themselves."

"I beg your most noble highness to pardon my ignorance. I will not offend again." Then to change the subject he said hastily: "I saw some Egyptians dance at Chicago, at the exposition, and also at Buffalo, and I suppose the slaves danced much like that in your day. They say that customs change little in those old places—that is—ah—in regard to such pastimes—" stammered the young man suddenly conscious that her painted eyes were flashing fire. She said haughtily:

"Do you refer to the dance called couchee-couchee? If you do, I will say that any slave that tried that on us of the old times would be short on heads so soon that she would not know what had happened to her." Then in a tone of disgust, she continued as if to herself:

"Now wouldn't that rock you to sleep?"

The manner in which this was said left no doubt in the mind of the young man that he had made a mistake, and he tried to pull himself together and said lamely:

"How did your illustrious highness learn to speak English so well? Why, you even seem to have learned our idioms."

"I have not lain in that museum so long for nothing, and all day and everyday there are men and women sitting around and snooping into things that do not concern them in the least. I cannot help hearing them, and their English is more remarkable for force than elegance, as you doubtless know. Now, in my time there was no difference between the language of the people and the slaves. We had a shorter vocabulary, and its very simplicity has made it possible for those who like to study into these things to read it.

"We were satisfied with what we had, but it seems to me that you are always seeking after new expressions, and I must say that I think our way was best. Yet, I find myself contaminated by the ungrammatical conversation of the throngs who frequent the place where I must stay. But unpleasant as that is, it is as nothing beside the conversation of the people who think they know it all, and their ignorance about things only six or seven thousand years ago is awful. To hear them flounder along and try to learn from what they see is bad enough, but nothing beside hearing those who think they know it all try to enlighten others. We can excuse one who is really ignorant and makes no secret of it, but the glib fellows who go on and talk of dynasties and Pharaohs—why they don't know the difference between a Pharaoh and a Sardanapalus. And, they, like everybody else, think that Cleopatra was the only queen in Egypt, and she was, as I said, so painfully modern. It is now too late to talk much and so I will say good-bye until next year. And do not forget that my mummy case is in the main aisle, near the archway leading to the second room. You cannot miss it, besides I will be there waiting for you. We can talk at our ease, and I do hope that some way can be devised by which I can be taken back to Egypt. Ah, dear Egypt, where rain and thunder come not and snow and ice are unknown."

"I will certainly be there if I am alive, and—beshrew me—(this sounded like the sort of thing one ought to say to a princess)—if I don't find some way to get you back to Egypt once more."

Then bowing to the princess he withdrew to make place for a man who had been standing there some time waiting to approach her.

"I wonder what has become of the Sociable Ghost?" thought the young man. He looked around, and seeing so many ghosts, and no sign of his friend, he suddenly felt himself grow very uneasy. What if he could not find his way out of this place? But his heart beat a little more regularly as the floor manager shouted loudly:

"Ladies and Gentlemen: We are about to be specially favored by hearing a song composed and sung by our friend, Capt. ———. He assures us that no one else has ever heard it, as he used to sing it only at night when at sea during storms. I have the honor—Captain ———."

Here the floor manager bowed and retired. The Captain proved to be the ghost who had brought the young man down here, and he took his place while the invisible music burst forth with a strong rush of sound that reminded the young man of the winds and waves in a storm at sea. The ghost began in a deep bass voice:

"With a hey and a ho for the white sea horses, Plunging and tossing on ocean's crest; With a hey and a ho for the warning they give us, The sailor's heart sinks low in his breast. They fight fierce battles there in the water, Till the surface is covered white with foam, The waters toss and are churned to lather That touches the edge of heaven's dome. Deep in the depths the shadows thicken, As gather the sharks from down below, And high in the heavens the storm clouds hover, As prancing fiercely the white horses go. Then in the black darkness we hark to the breakers, Dashing upon the bleak rocks their foam, Beaten to froth by the white sea horses, And none of the sailors reaches his home."

As this song was finished there was a regular salvo of applause, and in more ways than one, for the clapping of the fleshless hands was like the cracking of musketry. The ghost seemed to be pleased by the evident appreciation of his efforts, and sauntered over to the young man who expressed his pleasure so warmly that even an opera singer would have felt satisfied with such approbation and he requested permission to copy down the song, for sung in a grand and sonorous basso it had seemed to be a fine one.

When the last few desultory claps of applause at this song had died away the floor manager called out:

"Take your partners for a quadrille."

In a minute there was such a bustle that the newspaper man could scarcely hear himself think, but soon the sets were formed, and the whole immense place was filled with dancers, all in sets for quadrille. The music changed at the right moment, and the floor manager called out in stentorian tones:

"Salute your partners." And they all bowed in the regulation manner. Considering the almost universal poverty of wearing apparel, the ghosts danced and made a graceful appearance. There was scarcely enough cloth in good condition to have made a dress, but that fact did not seem to strike them as worth consideration. The manager cried:

"First two forward and back, cross over, balance to your partner, back to your place, all promenade." Continuing he led them through all the mazes of what he called allemand right, allemand left, all sashay, and so on until the whole was finished.

All the ghosts appeared to enjoy the free movement of the dance and to them it mattered little if the usual attire for such functions was conspicuous by its absence. The young man thought that as they had ghostly food and drink, furniture and decorations, perhaps they imagined their clothes as well. Then he suddenly remembered those tables. It struck him as curious that they had come and disappeared like things in some fairy tale.

As he watched the dancers, who were now waltzing, he thought of a curious experience that had happened to him a year ago. He had a ticket to go to Albany on the day boat, and he thought it would be a pleasant trip and a rest, for he had been working unusually hard for a fortnight. He had never made this trip and thought he would enjoy the beauties of the scenery, and incidentally, repose his mind.

The night before he was to make this trip he had a most vivid dream. He thought he was in a primeval forest and saw huge misshapen monsters, great prehistoric creatures, whose bones only now tell of their existence. Among them he saw a monstrous elephant covered with hair, and with immense tusks curved like those found among the eternal glaciers in far off lands. There were other strange animals and giants. As he went along he heard in one place a swishing like that of silks swirling in the dance, and a soft rhythmic sound, but nothing could he see until he suddenly turned a corner, and there was a room with hundreds of men and women dancing, but they all seemed to him to be dead. He turned to find someone who could explain this strange thing, but no one was near, and when he turned to look at them again they had all disappeared and an enormous gorilla stood in the place where they had been.

Then he awoke, and attended to his business of getting ready, and at the last moment hurried down to the boat. After the manner of busy men he reached there just as the bell was ringing, and when he went to hand in his ticket, he remembered that he had left it on the bureau, safely folded in a clean handkerchief. He said a word or two in appreciation of the situation and then said to himself that since he could not go to Albany he would go to Rockaway. He had never been there, though it was so nearby. The boat was just ready to start and the price for a round trip ticket but fifty cents.

The sail down was uneventful, and as it was a weekday and near the close of the season, he found very little to interest him there, so when he came to a museum, such as flourish at places like that, he decided to enter there to while away the time until the boat was ready to sail. As he entered the door, he saw the primeval forest of his dream, and every monster he found in just the same position. He thought he was living in the days long before man had entered into the history of the world. Wondering at this dream which had so curiously "come out," he suddenly found himself at the same place of which he had dreamed, where he had seen the dead folks dancing. He heard the same soft swish of silk, and the same subdued murmur and there were marionettes, hundreds of them all strung on invisible wires, and all dancing around in a mad revel that had something uncanny about it, particularly when taken in with the singular dream as a background.

Now he was down under Trinity Church looking at a revel far stranger, and he began to wonder if he were not a medium in spite of what the ghosts told him. He knew that the first experience was true, and he did not doubt that this one was equally so, and he thought that from now on he would take up the study of the unknowable and make an exhaustive research into all things relative to ghosts. Once before he had had a serious intention of writing a book on the subject of ghosts, authentic ones, but when he tried to get the matter together he found that the nearest he could come to what he wished to find was, that no one person not an avowed spiritualist, would admit having seen a real ghost, but nearly all knew of someone whose aunt or grandmother had heard of someone whose friends had thought they did see one. So he gave up that plan, but now he thought he might get notes enough to make a book on the subject, but then he might be injuring his plans regarding the princess. He compromised with himself by saying that if his plan for her deliverance failed he could then give the necessary time to the book. He regretted that he had not got his kodak along. What a chance it would have been to get that line of ghosts as they marched by, and what would he not have given for a snapshot at that "coon dance."

After the waltz the company broke up into groups and talked or promenaded around in couples, and it was a sight to remember forever to see the young lady ghosts as they walked or hung their heads and tried to look conscious at some tender compliment. The ghosts really had something of the semblance of life about them, for though they had no features left, nor eyes, there was some kind of inner light and a radiance which took the place of flesh. It was as though the soul had shed a soft light of its own over the fleshless skull and lent it something of its former appearance, and the thought came to him that perhaps these ghosts only saw the spiritual part of each other and just as he decided that such must be the case, as nothing else would account for so much that was otherwise unaccountable, there happened something to put all such ideas to flight, for the three ghosts who had looked upon the wine when it was red, seemed to have awakened under the impression that they were being neglected, and started a row, and began hitting out at any one in reach, be it man or woman, and so unexpected was the assault that the skeletons went down in heaps and lay there like so much new mown wheat.

The whole thing was so ludicrous that the newspaper man thought he must laugh or die. But he had been schooled not to laugh at the foolishness of others. That training stood him in good stead now, and he did keep his face straight by promising himself the luxury of a laugh the next day.

This control over his risibilities saved him from disaster when interviewing a great society woman one day. She told him that she could never bear to have any publicity, and really felt that the privacy of her home was sacred to her, and nothing about it ought ever to be put into any paper, while at that very moment he had her letter to his chief in his pocket, asking that a reporter should be sent to write a description of her house, which was one of the finest on Fifth Avenue. Her very virtuous indignation under the circumstances was so refreshing that the young man had found it a great and severe task to control his amusement, and ever since that experience he had been practicing self-control. If there is one thing more than another calculated to afford abundant practice in this line it is being a society reporter.

So now he even refrained from clapping his hands when the Sociable Ghost appeared with a bound, in spite of his sore toe, which the young man noticed was held up rigidly, notwithstanding the activity of the rest of the bony body. He laid the three flat with three well directed blows, and set the beholder to wondering what he could have done had he not been hampered by his troublesome foot.

When the three lay flat in a heap, he pushed them over into a corner with his well foot and told them to lie there and not to dare to move again until he gave them leave. One of them had lost one of his legs in the fracas and began to howl that he was all broken up. He begged someone to pull him out and get his leg for him. The Sociable Ghost said, as he rubbed his bony hands together:

"Say, oh, I say! This is fine! I have not had so much fun since I died. It brings back old times, and for one ineffable moment I thought I was back on my ship again and fighting out with a belaying pin at the mutineers. Oh, yes; I had a mutiny to deal with about every six months. It was fun. Danger? No, for the Captain always holds all the trump cards, and I was always ready to play them. By George, I was! And this brings it all back to me. Oh, I say; I must show you something a little out of the usual order. It is my wife's second husband. He is among the ghosts invited here from Derby, and I think it was a little cheeky for him to come here, don't you?"

"What are you going to do to him?" asked the young man with some natural curiosity.

"I am going to do just nothing to him. The poor chap has had troubles of his own with her—enough to balance any ill will I might have had. Now, my wife was, or rather is, for she is not dead yet, the kind of woman that what she wants goes, whether you want it to go or not. I was captain on board my ship, but she was the captain at home, and I was crew and cabin boy combined. Maybe I was a bit breezy toward my men when I got to sea again after a month or so on shore. Well: my wife had a portrait of me, and about every half hour she used to hale my successor up before it and tell the poor devil to look at it and see a man and, what one looked like. She dinned my virtues into his ears so much that at last the poor wretch died in self-defense."

"And where is the lady now?" asked the young man with interest.

"Somewhere in Boston, I believe. The last I heard of her she was giving my money away to the missionaries. I never had any use for missionaries, dead or alive. They come on board your ship, and the best you have is not too good for them, and they want to hold service every Sunday. I know a missionary as soon as I hear him speak. They always say Sabbath for Sunday, and babe for baby. There's lots of them down here."

For once the newspaper man forgot his tact, and said:

"I should think that you would have been glad to have them hold service for the sailors. I have heard that they are mostly amenable to religious instruction and guidance."

"Yah! Just stow that. The sailors don't want any of their salvation any more than the Chinamen, and it don't do any more good. You can't make a silk purse out of a pig's ear, and sailors are nothing more than living machines when they are on board ship. They are all right aboard ship, but they are no good on land, and whoever wants to do a good turn to a sailor wants to see that he gets a ship as soon as the voyage is done. They need knocking down every day with a marlinspike, and to get a taste of the rope's end every ten minutes, to give them a good appetite so they won't be forever grumbling about their grub."

The Captain might have continued indefinitely had not a polka struck up, and all the ghosts began to dance again. The dance of the marionettes came back to the young man's mind with insistent force, but he tried to hide his amusement.

To keep out of the way of the dancers the young man drew back and walked along close to the wall, and as he did so he was suddenly struck by the sight of a man stooping down so that he could eat out of a dish on the buffet without touching it with his hands. It was such a strange sight that he could not help making a mental note of it, and he really thought that he had not let the ghost see his curiosity. But it was not so, for the ghost turned and faced him and said sadly:

"Sir, I hope you will not think that my disgusting action is done through ignorance, nor even a lack of decency. I simply cannot eat any other way and I am very hungry. Owing to my affliction I could not present myself at the table with the others, and I thought that while all the others are dancing, I could satisfy my hunger without being noticed."

The newspaper man felt that here was another case of misery out of the ordinary, and he asked the ghost to tell him his trouble, and if it was anything that he could be of assistance in he would be glad to do all in his power. The ghost came to his rescue in a most unexpected manner, by suddenly holding up two mutilated stumps of arms. They had evidently been splintered off between the elbows and shoulders. By no effort could the poor fellow have been able to reach his mouth with either stump had he tried.

The reporter understood at once and felt so sorry for him that his usually ready tongue refused to form a word. He thought that it was more than probable that this accident had taken place in the Revolutionary war, and then he thought that that was too far away, and doubtless he must be one of the heroes of the Civil War. But the ghost as if answering a question, said:

"No, it was not in any war that my arms were smashed like that. If you would be so good as to help me get something to eat, I will tell you about it later. You can cut up some bread and meat and I must eat them right off the dish, and drink the best I can. It is very humiliating but I must bear it."

The young man took of the different viands and cut them into convenient pieces and then offered to hand them on a fork. If ghosts could shed tears of gratitude from their hollow eyes this one would surely have wept, so much was he touched by the action. He ate and drank with an excellent appetite, and when he had all that he desired, he said:

"Now, sir, I am at your disposal. I will tell you why it is that I am reduced to this condition and am obliged to eat like an animal. The story began in life, and it was not until I had been down here two years that this happened. I found an enemy and he it was who made me this pitiable object. The reason? Oh, I lived in New York in a handsome house of my own in Sixty-fourth Street, near the park on the East Side. I mention this, as the proximity has something to do with the story. That is, the big reservoir is there and that causes a higher pressure of water in the houses there than in almost any other part of the city. I lived there in peace and contentment and was something of a savant. So you can see that I am not altogether to blame for what follows. You know how all the houses are built, one beside the other. On the West side of my house was that of a man—well—we will call him Dinklespiel. That was not his real name—but it is good enough for him after the way he has treated me. Yes; I will call him Dinklespiel. Well; his front door was right beside mine. You could reach into his hallway over the low stone division. The next house on the East side was the whole width of the house away. Now, if Mr. Dinklespiel had lived in that house this would not have occurred.

"It so happened that our man who attended to all these things for me was out in the country getting the place in readiness for our annual flitting, and there was no one to clean the sidewalk and we had had coal in the day before. I admit that it would have been better to hire a man as my wife suggested, but somehow I felt like doing it myself, and that is how the trouble began."

Here the ghost appeared lost in reflection so the young man asked what would have been better left to a hired man. The ghost shook off his distraction and resumed.

"Why, I got the garden hose—well—I got the hose and washed down the sidewalk. I told you about the high pressure, and that was the cause of it all. I got the hose,—the hose—and dragged it up from the cellar, and told the girl to go down and turn the water on, when I whistled. This hose was bought to protect us from fire as well as to wash the sidewalk and water the grass in the back yard, and it had a nozzle one inch in diameter. It was a big hose, and when James took hold of it I always noticed that his face grew red as though he found it hard to hold. But I always thought that it was his ignorance that made him so afraid of it, and I was sure that I could manage it all right and I even rather prided myself on the showing I should make of the triumph of mind over matter. I had never tried to manage a hose before, and even now I should not, I think, have had any trouble if there had been no hole in the hose.

"I drew the hose up into the area way, and then whistled, and the girl turned on the water. Why, my dear sir, it nearly jerked me off my feet before I knew what had happened to me, and I held the nozzle straight up with both hands with all my strength, and pointed the stream upward so that I could get a little accustomed to it, and at the same time wash down the front of the house. Suddenly I heard a strange sound in the dining room where my little boy was looking at me, and saw that I had in some way for which I could not account nearly drowned him. I heard him run screaming up stairs to his mother, and then I thought I would go up the front steps and play on the second story windows, for it was summer and everything was dusty. Once I had learned to manipulate the hose, it was a delight. I had partially overcome my fear of it. Why, the violent stream rushed out like steam from an overheated boiler. It fairly screamed, the force was so great. Well, I played on the windows and then on the whole front of the house, and was enjoying my labor when I became aware that the servant was calling me from the area, and I bent over to hear her, keeping firm hands on the powerful nozzle that was twisting and trying to wriggle out of my hands all the time. Just as she opened her mouth—well—somehow she got very wet, and sat down in the middle of the area, and I turned around so that she should not think I was laughing at her miserable plight. Anyhow I had done enough up there and I intended to attack the dusty sidewalk, when my wife came to the front door and opened it unexpectedly just as I was in the act of turning, and somehow she received the full force of the stream right in the face and she went down like a shot. No one could blame me if in the face of this disaster I forgot and left the squirming hose to work its will and tried to raise her.

"She did not wait for me, however, but told me with a withering look to take that thing down cellar at once. I tried to explain, but she shut the door, and I started to obey her, but, sir, you could scarcely believe me, but I had lost control of the thing, and the more I tried to manage it the worse it got, and at last I found that there was a hole in the hose about a foot from the nozzle and that was running in opposition to the nozzle. I was wet to the skin, and the more I tried to get down the steps the worse it wriggled and twisted until I was at my wits' end to know what to do.

"At last I seemed to obtain a little command of it and was in the act of turning around to come down when I became conscious that there was a hearse and two carriages drawn up in front of my next neighbor's house, and before I could move the door opened and six men came out bearing a large coffin. I was struck dumb and almost blind, and did not know what I was doing, and—well—before I came to my senses every one of those pall-bearers was wet through, and the force of the water threw the flowers in every direction, and as if this were not enough the vicious stream hit the clergyman directly between the eyes and made him fall backward, and that was the reason that a number of people who had gathered to see a funeral at that unusual hour laughed. I was actually paralyzed with the whole thing and stood there helpless, trying to hold up the nozzle, not knowing that it was pouring floods into the vestibule of the dead man's house. Finally someone came up the steps and took the wretched thing away from me, and dragged it down to the area, and I scarcely knew enough to go after it.

"I have often thought that scientific men are not quite so well adapted to cope with the small things of daily life as those more in touch with mundane affairs. I was so distressed at my complete failure to master so simple a thing as a hose, and above all at the terrible disaster which had befallen me in the involuntary disrespect to my neighbor, that I was like a man dead.

"He had been away and died and was brought home for burial, and that was why the funeral was private and so early, for he was to be taken quite a distance for interment.

"So you can conceive of my distress, particularly as my wife did not feel willing to console me. On the contrary, she said quite a number of things which I am sure she would have left unsaid had she reflected. And I had to get her a new frock and one for the servant. After a while the neighbors stopped asking me impertinent things about my garden hose, and I was beginning to feel a little better about it when I fell ill and died.

"My funeral was marked by decorum, and everything passed off well. I was not sorry to come here for I had studied a little of everything else, and this being the unknowable held certain charms for me. I am of a philosophic nature, and very adaptable, and soon became quite content here, for if there are some drawbacks, there are some compensations too."

"What are they?" asked the reporter hastily, and not remembering that he was departing from his usual custom.

"Well, the greatest is—speaking generally, you know—that you can do no more wrong, and that you must progress, for nothing in nature can retrograde. We feel that we may advance in the scale of the great plan, and that our powers of evil are null, so we can hope. We do not know what we can hope for, but we are not hindered from hoping that there is something to hope for. But, the old desires, old frailties die hard and slow. But, all that is not the story of my misery. I came down here, and for a long time had no special trouble, and met in convention twice. I tried to study out all I saw, until one night I saw my neighbor whose funeral I had so unintentionally desecrated. He had been removed to another cemetery nearer and so was here as a guest.

"As soon as he saw me he acted as if he had been suddenly restored to all the vigor of life, and its animosity, for he followed me around all the evening until he found me in a corner studying the sculpture on one of the pillars. He knocked me down and jumped on me and kicked me until it is a wonder how I have a whole bone left. I could have tied any other bones on, but how could I tie without hands? I am sure that if he had given me the opportunity to explain how this unhappy affair had come about he would feel sorry that he was so rough. But he wouldn't listen and so he will never know."

"Yes, he will," said a voice right behind them, and as the reporter and the armless ghost turned together they saw another ghost, and he continued his unexpected conversation.

"I have heard your story, sir; and regret that I was so violent. I was exasperated beyond measure, as I was always a great stickler for strict decorum, and I was not to blame if I thought you did that on purpose."

The armless ghost was so affected that he would have fallen had not the other put his arms around him, and the chances for a complete reconciliation were so good that the reporter felt himself de trop and silently slipped away.

CHAPTER VII
THE GRAND BALL, CONVENTION AND END OF IT ALL

AFTER THE YOUNG MAN left the reunited friends he strolled along a little, and saw a man whom he had noticed two or three times on account of his height and the gloomy bend of his head. He stood with his arms crossed moodily over his breast and the reporter thought that perhaps there was some new phrase of misery indicated in this morose and gloomy attitude. The newspaper man edged along near him and bowing, said:

"This is a very pleasant reunion, is it not?"

"This is your first visit here, is it not?" answered the ghost somewhat irrelevantly.

"It is," replied he, thinking at the same time that it should be his last.

"I suppose you are greatly amused," said the ghost, who, the young man now noticed, was lame and limped painfully as he moved around to keep out of the way of the dancers.

"Well, not exactly amused," answered the young man doubtfully.

"We will say entertained, then," said the lame ghost. "You may have noticed that I do not dance, nor can I walk about like others. I do not think I would make a good figure. I have a misfit leg."

"I—I—beg your pardon," stammered the young man confused between curiosity and the fear of wounding the sensibilities of the ghost.

"Just so," resumed the ghost. "A misfit leg. Indeed I think it belongs to that young lady over there. But, as I see that she is provided with another, and I can manage to walk with this, I do not like to mortify her by mentioning it. You must admit that it would be very unpleasant for the young lady in company, now wouldn't it?"

"Would it be considered rude of me to ask how so deplorable an accident occurred?" asked the reporter with much interest.

"Certainly not," replied the ghost with a Chesterfieldian bow. "It was just this way. I was a Van Der Dam, and I have been dead a long time. First I was buried in a little graveyard away down town, and all the dead were moved from there to make place for the leather trade warehouses, and we were taken to another cemetery that was so far from the business section that we thought we were to stay there forever. But, in a few years we had to get up and go on again. In a short time that land was wanted for building purposes, and I was removed again to another place so far out that it was thought no one would ever require that land, I am sure you have seen that place, for it was where the old and well-liked Metropolitan Hotel was afterwards built. And just to think! The trustees of Trinity Corporation once had the offer of a gift of six acres of land on the corner of Canal Street and Broadway, and refused it, thinking the expense of fencing it too great, and that it was so far from the city that it would cost more for taxes than it was worth. What those six acres are worth now must mount up to millions.

"It was swampy, and we were not so very comfortable in this place, and we were not sorry when the order came to move us so they could build the hotel, which is but a memory now, with a big business house in its place. Many of my friends lie in unsuspected spots about that neighborhood yet.

"When the foundation for the hotel was dug many of us were discovered, and they took the bones and threw them into a cart in one big box, and held an inquest over the lot, and carted them away, and I do not know where they put them. I was moved from there to another place right in the heart of the retail dry goods district. We were put in a Protestant cemetery and right opposite was an old Jewish graveyard. No money consideration had ever been powerful enough to get this spot, nor any other Jewish cemetery, for business. Stores have been built up all around it. A friend of mine lies right under a water butt, for our graves were crowded as much as possible. That is a very unpleasant location. You must admit that."

The newspaper man did admit it, and condoled with the ghost, who kept his head bent always in sign of hopeless sorrow. He continued:

"When the march of progress reached as high as this place we had to get up again and go further so that a street could be cut through. A half brother of mine lost his head during the confusion resulting from this removal, and has never found it after that exodus. I suppose that head and the other fellow's body must have got together somehow, for my half brother found a head, but it does not fit, and the mental calibre cannot compare with that of my half brother."

"I should like to know, if it pleases you to tell me, which portion of a person's anatomy is the seat of the spirit or soul, or whatever you say when you wish to designate the human intelligence, and the spirit as I see it here tonight? I can scarcely formulate my meaning, but it seems to me that it is all that part of you that I see here tonight, and that seems to have all the intelligence of your living selves. Some of you appear to have all your faculties, can eat and drink and show a certain degree of physical force, and I cannot understand anything about it. Now, you mentioned the misfortune of your brother, and I am at a loss to know which is the most of him, his head that another wears, or the body which bears a head not his own. Which, in short, is your brother? The head without his body or his body without a head?"

"My dear sir, you raise a serious question there, and one very difficult to answer. All I can say is that I think my brother must be leading what you call a double life. His body acts as it always did, but there is a total lack of sequence in his conversation. I fairly hate to hear him speak. He is always declaring that the world is coming to an end. Now, what does he or any one know about the end of the world, when we do not know anything of the beginning of it, not even the scientists."

"The Bible says——" began the young man.

"Yes; and science says—Life is too short to go into those questions, and we might better talk of the present."

The young man took the hint and said:

"You were speaking of your several removals."

"Yes, and in each one I suffered, but it was after my removal from this last-mentioned place that the worst of my misfortunes befell me. We were moved to another burying ground about two miles further out of town. We were all beginning to feel at home and quite sociable, when it became necessary to grade the place and cut streets through. They cut the street through and left my coffin sticking out about two feet, and alas! I have never had two feet to stick out since.

"You see, my coffin was over a hundred years old, and it all crumbled away, and that is how I lost my foot. It was as solid and handsome a leg as you would wish to see, but the rascal who moved us broke up our coffins, and threw me into a dirty cart with a score of fellow sufferers, and were dumped into one hole, all in a heap. Somehow in the transportation my fine leg was lost, from the knee downward, and as if this was not enough, as I was the last one I had to take this and do the best I can with it. And, there sits the young lady, who, I am sure, has my leg, and this is probably hers, as I am sure that this is a woman's leg, it is so very small."

The newspaper man thought just as the ghost did, for not for worlds would he have dared to disagree with one of the ghosts down here in the bowels of the world. The ghost continued:

"It is impossible to portray the mental agony which one of my size and build experiences as he is obliged to go limping along in disgraceful manner, and I assure you that my everlasting gratitude would be given to the person who could relieve me of this hideous deformity."

"Why do you not go to the young lady and ask her frankly if she has not got a leg that does not belong to her? If so, she would doubtless be glad to make the exchange, and perhaps you will never have the opportunity again. You would know if it is really your leg, would you not? If her leg is too small for you your leg must be much too large for her, and she would appreciate the exchange."

"Young sir, I do not know how a young lady of the present day would take such a thing, but I assure you I would rather go through all eternity lame than to so sully the purity of a young girl's mind as to say leg to her, No, no; I must bear it as best I can."

"Oh, I say! What is the matter with my going to speak to her and see what she says? I will try to get the leg for you to try on, and if it is yours you can give me hers, and I am sure she will be as glad as you. I see she taps her own foot to the music, and I do not doubt that she is as anxious to dance as can be, and she cannot on account of this misfortune."

"If it could be so arranged that she would not know who it was that asked the change, I would be willing for you to try. That is, on condition that you will be as delicate as you possibly can, and we have not much time to work in for as soon as those who like to dance have enjoyed that pleasure we are to hold a short convention, and after that we go outside. But, it would be a great comfort."

The young man sauntered toward the young lady and noticed that she tried to hide the long leg and big foot behind her chair, and he felt emboldened, and addressed her:

"Fair lady, I beg your pardon in advance for what I am about to say, and I beg you to believe that I mean no disrespect, but as time presses and there are a few more dances on the programme, I must tell you the story of another's misfortune, so that you may understand the case."

Then he hastily told her the whole story of the lost leg, and by watching her intently he felt sure that he was right, and finally he asked:

"What would you suggest in order that those misplaced members might be restored to their rightful owners?"

"Oh, sir, it is a terrible thing, and I really do not know what should be done, other than that you should take the one I have and turn your back and take it from behind you, and carry it so, covered with your coat, and bring back mine in the same way, and manage so that no one shall see the transfer."

"Young lady, you are as sensible as you are lovely, and it shall be done as you say."

Saying that the young man threw off his coat and in a moment more had lifted it with something in it and made his way to the ghost in the corner waiting for him. He lost no time in dropping the offending leg as crabs drop theirs when they like, and tried the other. As he did so he cried joyfully:

"My friend, accept the thanks of a man who has nothing else to offer, but please go back to that young lady and when she is settled please offer her my thanks and hopes that she has suffered no inconvenience."

"I think it would be the fair thing if you asked her to dance with you since she has been so long deprived on your account."

"I couldn't, I really couldn't! I will wait here until you come back, and I beg you not to be long."

The young man hastened away on his important errand, and soon had the satisfaction of knowing that the young lady was very grateful to have her own long lost limb restored. She expressed herself so gracefully that the young man thought what a pity it was that she was dead. On plea of important business he left her, for he was afraid that she would expect him to offer to dance with her, but almost before he reached the ghost who was gleefully stamping his recovered leg, he saw her being led out for a polka. And she showed as keen a gusto as the good-natured ghost had with the pipe and the rest.

As soon as the young man returned the ghost who had now become quite cheerful said:

"My dear young friend, what a burden you have lifted from my heart! You have restored me my fine leg. What an outrage to permit any one to be so maimed."

"Had you no friends to protect you against such treatment?"

"No, for they are all dead, too, and so could not help me. They all lie in this churchyard, and probably will be left in peace, but if it is in human power to get this land where they lie they like the rest of us will have to make place for the living. The city will want the ground, and then it will be, 'Come along old bones, get up and travel, We need that ground to build on, and the dead have no rights beside the living.' "

"It is a great wrong," said a ghost who up to now had not joined in the conversation. "I will tell you a little of my experience, and that will show how little we weigh in the balance with dollars. In early days I lived in what was then the nucleus of Oakland, Cal. I had a little sister, and she died and was buried in the first cemetery laid out in that place. It was beautifully located on the banks of the estuary leading to Merrit's Lake, and under the great and evergreen old oaks, and there we left her to sleep. Scarcely a year had passed when a rich man came and the only place in all that county to please him was that little graveyard. He managed to get it for a residence, and all our dead had to be moved. Another place was chosen at the head of the lake, and they were all put there. I had married, and when my sister was removed my first-born was laid there too. About ten years later that place had grown too valuable to be given to the dead, and our dead were carried off to the foot hills, and now I am told that the time is not far distant when they will be taken on to the eternal Sierras. Now, my mother and father and other members of my family all lie there, but there is no one left to see that they are moved in a proper manner. I wish with all my heart we had all been cremated. We should all have been just haunts and not been obliged to drag old bones around, and run the risk of getting them scattered from Dan to Beersheba."

"I don't mind my bones at all," said the gloomy ghost who was now quite chipper, and he braced up and threw out his chest and smoothed his chin and looked grand—as grand as the nature of the circumstances would permit. "I used to be called a fine figure of a man."

The young man hastened to say that anybody with half an eye could see that he was still, for no one else took the slightest notice of him, and the young reporter was anxious to maintain the friendliest relations with all the ghosts. Then the ghost whose peace of mind he had been instrumental in saving, walked along with a stately stride in front of the young lady whose small foot had caused him so much anguish of mind. She had finished her dance by this time and had been sitting still. By some occult wave of sympathy she sent a sentiment of gratefulness to him, and in next to no time they were talking like old friends, but the painful subject of the exchange of bones was carefully ignored.

The ghost who had spoken in favor of cremation sat down beside the young man and seemed to wish to enter into conversation, and as the good-natured ghost had gone off again and was talking at a lively rate with some men who all had a sort of air about them which signaled them as seafaring men, he thought it best to let the ghost talk. To that end he listened intently. He continued his complaint:

"There are many more old and almost forgotten graveyards in this city, just as there are in every place of any age at all, and as there are still some relatives left alive they fight against allowing the places to be sold, but time flies, and some day these men will be dead too, and there will remain no one to defend them and the old bones will be carted off, and the worst is that we do get so mixed in these removals. See that man over there? He belongs to St. Paul's. I think this and that place will probably be kept inviolate, but who knows? But they are both so awfully crowded, and they kick like anything about letting any one be buried in either place now, and in fact no one can be buried there unless the family owns a vault.

"Now, I suppose that the families all think it is a great thing to have a vault, and go down a step ladder every time they want to pray and weep over their dead, but I tell you it matters little where we lie if we can only be left in peace. If we could all be cremated it would be better for all concerned, but the ashes should be scattered to the four winds, for, my young friend, time works many changes, and the needs of the living are greater than those of the dead. Right here in the vaults of St. Paul's that man over there in some changing about of bodies, lost one of his legs, and another was chucked into his coffin, so if you will notice, he has two right legs, and consequently the other man must have the two left ones."

The reporter did not exactly know how to take this, and looked at the bony face for something to show whether this was meant as a pun, or in simple earnest, but there was nothing to show that this was the melancholy remains of some humorist who had passed onward, so he said:

"Our lame friend said something about haunts. I did not quite understand it. I rather infer that they are something ethereal, having no bodies—or—bones," he added hesitatingly.

"Haunts, sir; just haunts. Invisible unrealities. There is nothing to them, and they just hover around. You may have heard of what some men say who are trying to show you that there is an odic force loose in the air, and they wish to prove that disembodied spirits can make use of this force to render themselves visible to experts."

"Meaning mediums?" questioned the young man hastily in his desire to have that question solved to his entire satisfaction, for he had a strong leaning to the belief in the occult powers of one medium in particular who had told him something he thought no one knew but himself.

"My dear boy, if anybody has told you that mediums or anyone else can materialize a spirit, that person is seeking to deceive you—possibly himself also. How is it possible to make something out of nothing? Unless it is that they make money out of the deception they practice? When I see the swindling wretches trying to make a fortune out of the grief of one who has lost a dear one, and who naturally turns to anything that promises to renew the tie that death has severed, I feel that I would willingly sacrifice all that I have gained toward my final release to proclaim the truth. No, friend, there is no means of communication between the living and the dead. I would there were!"

"Here tonight I have heard that the spirit can leave the body and go floating around. I see you here now, and suppose it means just the body as it is—as yours all are. Will you tell me how it is done."

"We can for a time drop off all material parts of ourselves, and then there is but the spiritual part and that is invisible, and can go anywhere by a thought.

I might explain by asking if you ever saw a flock of winged ants settle down on the ground and lift off their wings and leave them there. When I want to leave my body, or what is left of it, I just give a little and somehow I then leave the body behind and soar away. Soar after all is not the word to use, for the movement is more like a flash, and the movement is swift as thought, and nothing is so swift as that, not even lightning."

"Oh, tell me one other thing, Is there any truth in the theory that animals have souls, and live again after they have died? I loved a dog, and he was so faithful, so loving and above all, so intelligent that I have often wondered what became of my dog after he died. He was born as we are and died as we do, and in life he showed all the best qualities, such as honor, devotion, truthfulness and fidelity, and I could somehow never feel reconciled to think that a creature so good and so noble could be lost forever. Tell me, shall I ever see my dog again?"

"Rest assured that nothing good and true is ever lost to those who loved it because of its truth and goodness. I shall expect to find my own dog, and I am sure that dogs would not have to wait for their passports as we do, for they are not filled with evil of every kind on earth, and besides their suffering when in life must count for something."

At this moment there was a grand fanfare of trumpets, and the master of ceremonies stood on a chair and said in a loud voice:

"All present are invited to be seated as the convention is about to open."

The young newspaper man noticed all at once that while he had been talking with the man whose words about dogs had filled his heart with comfort, for he had loved that dog profoundly, and felt a great void left in his life when that of his dog went out—there had been a great change made in the room. The whole great hall had been fitted up with chairs and there was a platform. In front of the platform were chairs arranged for special guests, but it was but too evident that no provision had been made for reporters. This rather surprised him, and he asked the man next him how it was that the Press was not represented. The man looked at him a moment as we regard those that ask fool questions, and then he seemed to relent and answered:

"Sir, there are no newspaper men in this place. The Master who knows all things knows their sufferings on earth, and it must be that they get their passports right away, for there are none here. I had a chance to become a newspaper man, to get into newspaper work, but my family thought law more respectable, so here I am and may stay ten million years yet. Oh, yes, it is understood that we must remain here until the Master sees that we are sufficiently purified from earthly dross to enter into a higher sphere, where the most of our earthly sins and sorrows are forgotten. We are allowed to forget as fast as we have earned forgiveness. But, as I said, there are no reporters here but you, and it is understood that you are not to waste your time in writing out a report. Nobody would believe it if you did. Gee! I wonder what the editor of the paper up the street would say if you handed in your report of what you have seen tonight?"

The young man gave a short hysterical laugh as he replied:

"He would say, 'Go to the cashier and get what is coming to you. We publish nothing but facts.'"

Two or three of the ghosts who had heard this began to laugh derisively, and one or two made remarks not altogether to the credit of the editor's perspicacity, and there would doubtless have been more discussion had not the master of ceremonies rapped sharply for order, and said:

"All present are invited to take part in this convention which has been convened for the purpose of endeavoring to right several wrongs and to elect a master of ceremonies for next year. I think I am entitled to some repose. In fact I could not be induced to serve another year in this capacity."

"I wonder if anyone asked him to?" whispered one ghost to another. The reporter looked around to see the speaker, forgetting that he would not know anyhow. His surprise was great to observe that all the women ghosts were seated in a gallery that he had not noticed before.

The women were talking with animation among themselves and paid scant attention to the proceedings below. They grew so animated once or twice talking of the fashions which women still of the world were wearing, and telling of the clothes they used to have that they had to be called to order twice. The master of ceremonies rapped for order, and said:

"I move that Mr. Alexander Hamilton be invited to act as chairman for this meeting."

The bishop immediately stood up, saying angrily:

"I object! Mr. Hamilton has been chairman often enough. I move that someone else has a chance this generation. Besides we want new blood, new ideas."

"That lets you out, then," said a ghost down the aisle.

The bishop was too angry to answer, and sat down indignantly. Another ghost said:

"What is the matter with the general? I see our fighting general here, and I should like to remark that Mr. Hamilton is not the only peach upon the bough. If the general is too modest I move that the chairman should be someone who has suffered by the wrongs we are trying to have righted. Mr. Hamilton is sure that he will never be removed from here, or if he is it will be with befitting ceremonies, and he cannot be expected to feel as do those who have been moved around until they have no fixed abode, and in consequence are called tramp ghosts. Of course the general will always be honored in death as he was in life, still I think he ought to be our chairman."

All eyes, or rather, heads were turned toward a medium-sized ghost who stood up, and it was easy to recognize the military bearing as he replied:

"Gentlemen" (for the whole audience had applauded his name), "I am proud to know that you like me well enough to choose me, but I am not used to this kind of fighting. Anything else that I can do I shall be pleased to do."

Saying this he sat down and so decided was his movement that no one thought of asking him to reconsider.

Everybody cheered him except the women, who were vexed that they had been obliged to go upstairs. The master of ceremonies grew desperate and said:

"We will ask Mr. Van Der Dam to preside, with the approbation of the company."

The company for the most part appeared satisfied, though one or two said something about not liking to have a tramp ghost put above them. He took his place modestly and began:

"Friends and fellow citizens; I am here before you to see if some way cannot be devised to let the people above ground know our wrongs, and ask them to fix it so that every cemetery shall be made enduring and that no matter what are the demands of grasping people, these places shall be kept inviolate, and devoted sacredly to their purpose, or, if that cannot be done, then let us all be cremated, not only those who may die, but also those who lie in places that may become necessary to the living. What I mean is that when any old cemetery is to be moved, let them cremate the bones instead of throwing them into some filthy old cart all in a heap. We have all known what one can suffer under this sort of treatment. It is time that it was stopped. Of what use is all our boasted civilization if the dead are obliged to wander around without coffins? Yes, and half of them without more than half their bones. No one seems to care if they get mixed up and lost, or what becomes of them. Something ought to be done. I have no more to say."

Saying that he took his seat, and all the ghosts applauded him, though one or two exchanged opinions in whispers, saying that though what he had said was true it wasn't practical. Another ghost had just risen to his feet and opened his jaws—all the ghosts just wagged their jaws when they spoke—and said Fellow—when there was a sound of a silvery bell in the distance, yet its tones vibrated sweetly through this vast place. In an instant all was changed. The seats were gone, and no vestige of them remained. All the ghosts had changed too, and instead of being gay and festive, they looked sad and downcast, and their heads were bent and their whole air was one of intense dejection.

The young man asked one of the ghosts what the matter was, and he replied simply "penance," and fell into line as if to go somewhere. The heart of the intrepid reporter sank into his boots as he looked around for the ghost who had invited him down here and failed to see him anywhere. Finally, just as he had lost all hope he felt a light touch on his shoulder, and turned to see who it was, and there he stood, grinning.

"Did you think I had deserted you? Well, you need not have been alarmed, for there is one thing ghosts don't do, however much they may have deviated in life, and that is, they tell the truth. And I told you I would come in time.

"We are now going outside, and you shall see how some of us have to work to get our passports, and it may be a lesson for your future guidance. And, yes, I have thought out how you may arrange about the rum. It will be more to your interest to go up to the museum, and I never was one to interfere with an appointment with a lady, so go up there by all means, but if you can and will, why you can stop and just tuck the bottle and tobacco and pipe under the stone where I sat when we first made each other's acquaintance. I have heard that there are now to be obtained waterproof matches, and if that is so I would suggest them, for think what a disappointment it would be not to be able to light the pipe after all! I shall think about it the whole year, and I do not know how I could bear such a terrible disappointment."

The young man felt a glow of shame to think that he had thought more of his own benefit than of his promise, and as he thought the good-natured ghost said:

"My dear boy, do not worry over that. You did quite right, and if you can help that poor princess you will be doing a meritorious action. She may be, and probably is able to do all she asserts. I am sorry that I do not know where there is any treasure, but I will look around and make inquiries, and if you have time to see me at our next anniversary just for a moment I shall be only too glad to tell you."

"I wish to see you again, not only on the next, but also all other anniversaries, as long as it shall be possible, but I have learned too much since I came down here tonight to ever care for money again save for what good I can do with it. One thing I have had in my mind for a good while, a desire born of things I have seen in and around newspaper offices and among other publishers. There is no room for old writers. The cry is always for new thoughts, fresh ideas and the finish and depth of thought which the elderly writers bring are nothing beside the sensational work of the young man. I have thought sometimes when I saw the reporters rushing off copy under high pressure only intent on getting something so sensational that it would make even the managing editor hold his breath, that that is not the kind of thing that ought to be written. The older men would hesitate to father such stuff, and because they have culture and conscience enough to do better and more worthy work no one will buy it. What I would like to do is to found a weekly paper where every contributor should be at least sixty years old. It might be considered slow by those accustomed to the sensational journals of today, but it would be good mental food, and it would also give the old men a chance to live."

"In that way we might learn from the wisdom of age, in your paper, and be cheered by the sallies of youth in the others. Is that it?"

"Exactly. But I see no chance of being able to do this, unless something now entirely unexpected happens."

"I will try and see if I can't manage to interest some of the ghosts down here and we can possibly find the means to help you, for while we naturally are obliged to leave all wealth behind us, we may be able to locate hidden treasure for you or at least a mine."

"I may never be able to carry out my plan, but this I can promise you, that if I ever see a body about to be moved I will try to see that it is comfortably fixed. And, I think I shall always be a little more careful what I do, and if you will allow me to say it, I shall always feel grateful to you for bringing me down here tonight. As long as I shall live and am able I shall make it a point to come here every anniversary of this night, bringing with me such creature comforts as I think may prove acceptable."

"You said that before, but I thank you again," replied the ghost, at the same time taking his hand and shaking it with a fervor not to be expected in one so long dead, and in the world of spirits.

By this time the assembly had begun to pass out of the underground place, and many of the ghosts—in fact all of the invited guests and tramp ghosts faded away, and the young man rubbed his eyes to see where they had gone. All that he could determine was that they had been there and were gone.

They stood in the graveyard again, and the tramp ghost of Mr. Van Der Dam, the man whose leg the reporter had been the means of restoring, bid him a sorrowful good-bye. He shook his hand until the young man wished in his heart that the ghost were a little less demonstrative. He wished him the best of good fortunes, and saying that disappeared so suddenly and completely that it made him dizzy.

He now became aware of a subdued murmur that passed all over the place. The sociable ghost stood near him by the side of the stone from under which he had exuded, so to speak, earlier in the night. He suddenly dropped to his knees, regardless of the pebbles which might have hurt the fleshless bones, and began rubbing the stone actively, while there were sounds of moaning and sobbing heard all over the place, and in the semi-darkness the young man saw forms crouching down by the different headstones.

There was a sound like scouring and scraping, and then bright, livid lines of light quivered and trembled along the different tombstones in the form of words. At last the young man could not control his curiosity any longer and asked the ghost to tell him what it all meant.

"Why just this. We have to come out of our graves every year and read our own epitaphs. Then we have to write what we deserved in truth. I assure you it is not a pleasant task, and we all wish that our sorrowing friends would only be so very kind as not to put anything but our names upon the stones.

"Nobody cares anyhow what is on another's gravestone, and if any stop to read it it is simply to make fun of it. To read our own epitaphs and know how little we merit the extravagant praise there is one of our sharpest pangs. When we have shown a proper degree of shame and remorse over them, then we are allowed a short time in which we can endeavor to efface the lying records. We are given the privilege of scouring them with sandpaper and holystone. We hope that when the undeserved epitaph is all worn away we may be given our passports.

"I suppose you have noticed how much sooner a gravestone wears away than a building stone? Now, here is a granite monument, and down there, across the street, is a building with the whole front of the same stone, quarried in the same year, some of it the same week. The house is as good as ever, but look at the stone in the monument. That tells the story.

"See that woman down there trying to rub out the lies that her family put there. I wonder why it is that the survivors seem to feel constrained to put all that stuff on the headstone?"

"I was just wondering," said the young man, "how it would be if any ghost should outlive his or her stone. I heard there was a great fire here once that destroyed many of them. And I know of a baker who took three or four stones from a cemetery to bake his bread on. The names were smoothed off, and I cannot exactly understand how it all is. Is it that the dead are held for the sins of their survivors in putting all the false, if fond, words there?"

"No, not at all. If it were not this it would be something else."

All this time the ghost was rubbing away at his own headstone with greater vigor than one could have expected, and as the young man looked at it the ghost said:

"Pretty tough work, but I have succeeded in rubbing out nearly half this letter in only sixty years. This word is 'charitable,' and I never gave a cent to anybody in charity. I told you I would explain. Well, here is my epitaph, 'In memory of Captain, a pious and benevolent man, whose noble and upright character, calm demeanor and charitable heart endeared him to all who knew him. He passed away, leaving a sorrowing spouse to whom he was devoted, in the surety of a life above. He was captain of the ____, and engaged in the Liverpool and West India trade." This is a pretty mess to fix up over your head, now isn't it? Piety and the West India trade didn't go together in those days. Calm demeanor! Huh! They called me 'Old Hurricane.' And I was worse than a pirate, for I was in the slave trade. It is all over now, and the evil I did can't be undone, but though it may seem long, there will come a time when I—even I—shall have become fit for my passport.

"But let me tell you, young man, and try and remember what I say, if the living only knew what the dead do there would be a deuced sight less wickedness in the world. You know that the preachers have always told us that no matter what we had done of evil, we would be sure of complete pardon and forgiveness for it all, even murder, if we only could say that we accepted and believed what they told us. So many just went on and played merry hell, and at the last minute sent for a sky pilot and repented, and were assured by the clergy that they were saved and sure of heaven.

"Now, young man, don't you take any stock in that at all. Don't forget for one minute that when you do a thing that your inner self feels to be wrong, you are going to pay for it, and you won't pay the debt in counterfeit coin, either. If people only knew enough to understand that that very inner sense of what is right and wrong which we call conscience is the law we should follow closer than the laws made by men, they would be coming nearer to obeying the commands of the Master than they do. Unhappily we do not know that until it is too late, but the Master knows our motives, our ignorance, the pressure of outside influence, temptation and environment, and it is safe to trust to Him, for knowing all and being our Creator He knows and pities our weaknesses, and compassionately gives a chance to—and—so—well we can—my dear sir, I can say no more now, for the time is up. Good-bye till next year—good-bye."

As the Sociable Ghost said this, a bell began to ring somewhere. At this sound all the ghosts sank out of sight so swiftly that all the young man could remember was that the good-natured ghost had waved his bony hand. The change had taken place so rapidly that the young man sat and rubbed his eyes to see if they were open. As the sound of the bell grew louder, night began to fade before the early dawn.

The young man looked around and found that he was seated on the very slab where he had been when he had first seen the Sociable Ghost. He almost convinced himself that he had had a vivid dream. He might have come to believe it fully if he had not found the tobacco paper entirely empty and the matches all burned. And there was not a drop of whiskey left.

And as if these facts were not enough, he noticed that it had rained heavily during the night. There were pools and puddles of water in all the depressed places. The trees dripped water, but his clothes were perfectly dry. He was and is still convinced that this was not the baseless fabric of a dream, but the reality. He fully intends to keep his two unusual appointments next year, and try to fulfill his promises.

One good thing came out of this night's experience, and that is that his heart has ceased aching in that dreadful way about the marriage of the girl he loved. In the light of all he learned it became a chastened sorrow, and he could even think of it as something that had happened years ago—many of them—and we all know that when a grief reaches that point it is really cured.

But he never found the little cat, nor the dog, and his conscience still twinges whenever he thinks of his wanton cruelty in bestowing that unmerited kick on the dog, and throwing the stone at the cat.

www.ingramcontent.com/pod-product-compliance
Lightning Source LLC
Chambersburg PA
CBHW011438170626
46808CB00009B/3094